A Deadly Del

A Chocolate Centered Cozy Mystery Series

Cindy Bell

This is a work of fiction. The characters, incidents and locations portrayed in this book and the names herein are fictitious. Any similarity to or identification with the locations, names, characters or history of any person, product or entity is entirely coincidental and unintentional.

All trademarks and brands referred to in this book are for illustrative purposes only, are the property of their respective owners and not affiliated with this publication in any way. Any trademarks are being used without permission, and the publication of the trademark is not authorized by, associated with or sponsored by the trademark owner.

ISBN-13: 978-1519340191

ISBN-10: 1519340192

Table of Contents

Chapter One 1

Chapter Two 19

Chapter Three 41

Chapter Four 58

Chapter Five 77

Chapter Six 91

Chapter Seven 105

Chapter Eight 127

Chapter Nine 138

Chapter Ten 149

Chapter Eleven 157

Chapter Twelve.. 172

Chapter Thirteen 183

Chapter Fourteen 203

Chapter Fifteen 212

Chapter Sixteen 223

Chapter Seventeen 236

Chapter Eighteen 251

Chapter Nineteen 259

Decadent Chocolate Cake Recipe 264

More Cozy Mysteries by Cindy Bell 268

Chapter One

“You have to use the cinnamon stick to stir it, otherwise it just isn’t the same.” Charlotte moved her hand in a slow, swirling motion. The graceful flick of her wrist made Ally smile. Though her grandmother was older, and her skin showed a few wrinkles and other signs of age, her dexterity had not diminished. She made everything she did look like it had been choreographed.

“I see.” Ally tried to mimic the movement with her own cinnamon stick. Unfortunately, she had not inherited her grandmother’s grace or coordination, and the liquid splashed more than it swirled. As she watched the brown liquid in her mug settle into a languid whirlpool her muscles relaxed.

Since Ally had moved back home to the cottage that she shared with her grandmother as a child, her life had changed immensely. But then the past year had been filled with changes. She divorced a man who did not love her, she left behind a life that no longer suited her, and she took on the responsibility of being a full-time employee of Charlotte's Chocolate Heaven. Everything slowed down. It was a bit like traveling back through time, and also a bit like landing on a familiar, yet foreign planet. "You know, I've been thinking. It's going to be pretty lonely here all by myself."

"You could get a housemate." Charlotte shrugged and took a sip of her coffee.

"I could. But I'd much rather have you as a housemate than anyone else."

"Ally, we've been over this. It's time for me to move on. I've been looking forward to this. Besides, you're young, you don't need an old lady hanging over your shoulder all day."

"Oh, there's nothing old about you, Mee-Maw, nice try."

"I'm not much of a lady either." She grinned. "I'm looking forward to getting to know a few of those handsome, single men."

Ally laughed, then took a sip of her coffee. She looked fondly across the kitchen table at her grandmother. "Promise me that when you move to Freely Lakes we'll still have cinnamon flavored coffee every morning."

"I promise, dear. Don't worry, you won't be able to get rid of me. I have to say though that I am looking forward to all of the activities and fun that I will have once I'm settled there. I was a little surprised that a few of my friends moved away, but that just gives me a chance to make some new ones."

"That's why I think this weekend will be good for both of us. You'll get to meet some of your neighbors, and I'll get to check things out to make sure it's good enough for you."

"You're too good to me, Ally. Try not to forget that I don't require much to be content. Four walls and a bed will do."

"Maybe not, but you do deserve the best of everything." Ally reached across the table and gave her grandmother's hand a light squeeze. It was hard to believe that so many years had passed since the time when Ally was faced with the loss of her mother. Her grandmother had filled her mother's shoes in the best way she could, and although Ally missed her mother, she did not feel as if she had missed out on her love.

"Oh pish, you're biased." Charlotte rolled her eyes. "The important thing is we need to get me packed up!"

"Let's visit the place first, then we'll get into the heavy packing." Ally pursed her lips. She was not convinced that Freely Lakes was the best place for her grandmother, and wouldn't be until she knew for certain that it was safe. Not that she had much say about whether her grandmother moved there or not. When Charlotte set her mind to something it was best not to argue.

"Fair enough." She glanced at her watch. "We have to get going, if we're going to open the shop on time. I guess these coffees will have to be to go."

"I'm on it!" Ally jumped up and began the

process of transferring the coffee into travel cups. Once they were prepared she turned to see her grandmother already at the front door.

"Let's go, you can't be late for your first official day of being a manager!"

"All right, all right, just let me feed Peaches." She grabbed a can of cat food and popped the lid open. As soon as the subtle pop of the can filled the kitchen, an orange cat raced into the room. A pot-bellied pig raced in right after her.

The cat screeched as the pig rushed in behind her. Peaches jumped up onto the counter and skidded across the freshly cleaned surface.

"Peaches, it's okay." Ally reached out and stroked her back. "Arnold, this isn't for you!" Ally grinned. She filled the cat's bowl with cat food and then set it down on the floor beside her water bowl. Arnold sat back on his haunches and looked up at Ally with wide, pleading eyes.

"All right, all right, I'll get you something, too." Ally reached into the cabinet and pulled out a bag of pig feed. She sprinkled some on a mat on the floor. Arnold snorted and huffed his way over to the food. Within mere seconds the food was gone. He snorted up at Ally for more.

"That's enough, you have to keep a trim figure, little fellow." Ally reached down and patted the top of the rather stout pot-bellied pig's head. Peaches paced along the counter. She swished her tail sharply back and forth.

"Oops, I don't think Peaches appreciates having company for breakfast." Charlotte winked.

"Poor guys. They're not used to having to share their home." Ally scratched the top of Peaches' head with a light, soft touch. "I love you." She placed a peck on the top of the cat's head. Peaches rubbed her cheek against Ally's, then hopped down from the counter. She swished her tail saucily through the air as she walked away from Arnold. Arnold snorted and sniffed his way under the kitchen table.

"Don't worry, they'll learn to get along. It's always the ones that fight it the most that fall the hardest." Charlotte smiled at Ally. Ally raised an eyebrow.

"A love affair between a cat and a pot-bellied pig? Now that's strange."

"Quite." Charlotte laughed and pulled open the back door. "Ready?"

"Absolutely." A flutter of pride caused Ally's cheeks to flush as she followed after her grandmother. As a little girl she had spent hours curled up behind the counter of her grandmother's shop. The smells of chocolate, toffee, and various spices had enchanted her mind with dreams of the decadent chocolates she would get to taste. Never once did she imagine that she might one day be in charge of making those chocolates. Ally looked forward to her grandmother teaching her all of her secrets. Charlotte looped her arm through Ally's as they walked down the street towards the shop. Blue River was a small town so Charlotte very rarely drove. She didn't even own a car anymore, she would just use the van they used for deliveries at the shop if she needed to drive anywhere.

"Look at that, the convenience store has soda on sale. We should stock up on some in case any customers ask for it." Ally pointed out the sign to Charlotte as they walked past it.

"Ugh, no thank you. Soda would ruin the taste of the chocolates. You have to remember, Ally, our customers don't just come into the store for tasty treats, they come in for the experience. It must be just as decadent and intricate as the sweets that we offer them."

"You're absolutely right. Who would ruin chocolate with soda anyway?" Ally shrugged.

"You would be surprised what people do to chocolate."

***

When they opened up the shop Ally was greeted by the lingering aroma of chocolate. It had a way of permeating everything. She closed her eyes for a moment and inhaled the smell, as she had for so many years. She and Charlotte fell easily into the routine of opening up the shop. They spent about twenty minutes making sure all of the counters were wiped down, the register was open, and the floors were swept. Then Ally walked up to the sign on the front door and turned it from closed to open. She smiled to herself at the thought of this being her new job.

Although, when Ally had originally graduated from college she had taken a chocolatier's course because she had wanted to eventually own her own chocolate shop, this was certainly not how she had imagined her life unfolding in recent years. She found herself surprisingly content. She was touched that her grandmother trusted her enough to give her a key and to allow her to work in the shop alone. As far as she knew, no one else had a key.

"Okay, let's get to work. I want to make sure that there are plenty of chocolates for everyone tomorrow. Have to make a good first impression." Charlotte took out some empty molds. "Can you line these with chocolate and then make the fillings, please. I'll help and serve customers as well."

“Sure,” Ally said as she started filling the chocolate molds. Ally helped her grandmother make the fillings while the molds were setting.

Once they were done Charlotte took some of the chocolate lined molds out of the fridge and placed them on the counter. “I want these to be raspberry filled. And also it’s time I taught you the recipe for the walnut, expresso cream milk chocolates!”

“Great, I can’t wait!” Ally’s eyes widened. Ally still loved learning her grandmother’s delicious recipes. As her grandmother walked her through the steps to create one of her favorite chocolates, Ally savored every moment.

“Will you place the leftover expresso cream in the fridge, we can make some more chocolates another day. That’s enough for now,” Charlotte said.

“Sure.” Ally walked over to the fridge.

“All right, now that is settled we can work on the solid chocolates while those set. Do you want to do those on your own?”

"Okay."

"Just watch the double boiler, it gets hot fast. I'm going to serve the customers and put together some orders for delivery out front, okay?"

"All right." Ally nodded and set about preparing the solid chocolates. As she did she caught sight of a face in the window. It startled her at first. One of the draws of her grandmother's shop was the window that looked right into a section of the kitchen from the main shop. Charlotte felt it gave the community a chance to take part in the chocolate making, and that it also kept their cooking practices transparent and accessible to anyone that was interested. Over time the window had become a popular place to spend a few minutes when you bought some chocolates. Ally smiled at the woman in the window and then tried to focus on the chocolates.

A few minutes later Ally stirred the chocolate in the double boiler and gazed at the subtle bubbles that attempted to form. She created a smooth whirlpool before they could pop. With one hand she turned down the heat, and with the other she continued to slowly stir the chocolate. She forgot all about the window and whether she had an audience. The smell of chocolate and the heat of the stove worked together to make her very relaxed.

As Ally stirred, her mind drifted from childhood, to adulthood, to what might come in the future. She was so engrossed in her thoughts that she didn't even notice that she had poured the chocolate into the molds. Lost in a trance she created the chocolates on autopilot.

By the time she slid them into the refrigerator, she had been working for over an hour. She blinked with surprise as she snapped the door shut. A quick glance around at the mess she had left behind was clear proof that she had indeed made the chocolates. With a short laugh she began cleaning up the mess.

"Ally!" Charlotte stuck her head into the back room. "Are you done?"

"Yes." Ally opened her mouth to describe the

strange trance she had fallen into when the light above her head went out.

"Oh no," Charlotte said. "I don't think I have a spare light bulb." She walked over to the storage cupboard to check. "We don't have any. Can you run to the convenience store and pick some up and while you're there can you also get some antifreeze for the van, please? I keep forgetting to pick it up. I'll take care of the clean-up, all right?" She handed Ally the empty light bulb box she had kept, so she could get the right one.

"Sure, no problem." Ally took off her apron and stepped out through the back door.

Ally walked a few blocks down to the convenience store. It was pretty busy, with lots of people buying several bottles and twelve packs of soda. Ally picked up the light bulb and then the antifreeze and waited patiently for the line to dwindle. The woman behind the counter worked hard to keep up with the customers. When Ally arrived at the front of the line she set the items on the counter.

"And how much soda?"

"None today." Ally smiled. "Just these."

The woman nodded without even looking up. She rang up the items and gave Ally the change. "Next!"

Ally grabbed the items and made her way back through the crowd. She recognized a few of the faces, but many of the people that lived in the town now were unfamiliar to her. Ally knew that she would get to know them while running the shop. When she returned to the shop her grandmother had taken the chocolates out to package them.

"I'll just replace the bulb and then I can do that." Ally smiled and left the antifreeze on the back step to fill the van with later. She got the step out of the cupboard and climbed on it to replace the bulb. Once she was finished and had put the step away she pulled her hair back. She washed her hands thoroughly and pulled on some gloves. Then she began placing each chocolate into its own little nest in the box. She repeated the process for all of the chocolates they had made.

Ally sealed the last box and tied a gold and green ribbon around it to match the gold writing on the boxes that her grandmother had chosen. To her, the colors represented friendship and the future of her grandmother's social life at Freely Lakes. Although she still wished Charlotte would stay at the cottage with her, she understood why her grandmother had to move on. She wanted her freedom, as much as Ally was afraid of hers.

"All set for tomorrow." Ally placed the boxes on a shelf and turned to her grandmother. "I'm just going to clean the windows and head home. Why don't you go by the diner to get something for dinner?"

"Good idea. They have their turkey soup on special tonight, does that sound good?"

"Oh yes, especially if you get some of those amazing rolls."

"Will do." Charlotte smiled.

Ally stepped outside armed with window

cleaner and a squeegee. She plugged some earbuds into her phone and stuck the earbuds into her ears. As one of her favorite songs blasted into her ears she sprayed a generous amount of cleaner onto the window. The more the beat pumped, the more she shifted her hips from side to side. Without realizing it, she began to dance as she sprayed the window. Her sprays were a bit more enthusiastic than needed. As she swung her hand to get the top corner of the window, she felt her elbow connect with something solid and soft at the same time. She turned to see Luke Elm only a few feet away from her. He smiled as he rubbed his forearm.

"Hello, to you too, Ally." His bright, hazel eyes met hers. Ally tugged the earbuds out of her ears.

"I'm so sorry, Detective, I didn't mean to hit you."

"Detective?" He grinned. "I thought we were at least on a first name basis."

"Sorry, Luke." She smiled.

"Hey, I don't penalize anyone for having

passion about their work."

"I was enjoying myself a little too much." Ally ducked her head as her cheeks grew hot. Of all the people that she would prefer not to see her window-washing-dance, Luke was definitely in the top three.

"Not at all." Luke's grin faded into a subtle smile as he studied her. "I'm just sorry I interrupted. Honestly, I came over here because I couldn't tell if you were dancing or waving to me. Now I see, you were dancing."

"Yes, I must have looked ridiculous."

Luke shook his head a little. "No, you looked beautiful." He blushed slightly as he ran a hand back through his light brown hair and brushed it back from his eyes. "I'll let you get back to work. I just wanted to say hello."

"Hello." Ally smiled. She wanted to say something clever to hold his attention, but instead she said the first thing that popped into her head. "Do you want some chocolate?"

“I’d better not, don’t want to spoil my dinner.” Luke winked at her then walked away. Ally wasn’t sure what to think of the detective. He was a transplant from the city, and though he acted like a perfect gentleman, Ally could sense that he was out of his element. She popped her earbuds back into her ears and returned to the window.

Chapter Two

That night after Ally shared a delicious meal with her grandmother, she retreated to her room. As usual Peaches followed right along behind her. Ally's ex thought it was odd that she could have such a strong connection to a cat. But to Ally, Peaches was a friend, her best friend. It didn't matter to her that they were different species. As soon as she sat down on her bed, Peaches jumped right up beside her. Ally stroked her orange fur.

"You will not believe who saw me dancing like an idiot today." Ally laughed. "I guess Luke got quite an eyeful. He said I looked beautiful, but I think he was just being polite. I'm not sure that he will ever look at me the same way again." Peaches nestled her hand and meowed softly. "I know, I know, you love me no matter what." Ally smiled at her cat. Peaches always calmed her down. She decided to let go of the embarrassing moment and focus on the next day. In her mind she began to list all of the questions she wanted to ask the staff of Freely Lakes. She also decided that the next time she saw Luke she would ask him about any crimes in that area. The retirement community was still in Blue River, but it was on the border of the neighboring town of Freely. Freely Lakes got its name from the cluster of three lakes on which it bordered.

Even though it was only five minutes away, that didn't mean that it wasn't a target for criminals. Ally fell asleep that night with a solid plan in mind for ensuring that her grandmother's new home would be safe and comfortable. That plan was ripped right out of her mind when her grandmother burst into her room the next morning.

"Ally, Ally, we overslept! We have to get going. I don't want to be late! First impressions matter!"

"Huh? Okay. Wait, I'm getting up." Ally struggled to her feet with sleep still clinging to her senses.

"Hurry, we still have to get the chocolates!"

Ally had a quick shower and rushed to dress,

then made sure both Arnold and Peaches had food for the day. Once that was taken care of she grabbed her keys.

"Ready, Mee-Maw?"

Her grandmother stepped out into the hallway in a sleek, silver blouse paired with a fluted, purple skirt. The combination of color accented her eyes, her figure, and the bright smile on her lips. It was unusual for Charlotte to wear something so smart and for the first time Ally realized that her grandmother really was looking forward to more of a social life.

"You look gorgeous."

"Why, thank you." Charlotte smiled. "Are we ready to go?"

"Mm, just let me gulp down this cup of coffee." Ally guzzled the liquid without even adding a drop of milk. The drive to the shop was fast. Ally's heart pounded from the chaotic morning and the fact that despite the black coffee she was still trying to wake up.

"You stay in the car, I'll grab the chocolates." Ally hopped out of the car and rushed to the front door. She fumbled with the keys as she attempted to open the lock. As she finally slid the key into the lock the morning sunlight played off the large front window of the shop. Despite the fact that Ally had spent so much time cleaning the windows the day before she could see several smudges on the surface of the window. She wiggled the key and finally got the door open, but there wasn't time to clean the windows again. If they wanted to make the open house they had to get there fast. She rushed inside and grabbed the chocolates off the bench. On the way out she was careful to make sure she locked the door. She returned to the car with the chocolates and handed them to her grandmother.

"Let's roll!" Ally smiled as she turned down the road that led to Freely Lakes. "I'm ready to see what this place has to offer."

"Me, too!" Charlotte grinned.

A large bunch of balloons sailed high in the

air, tied down to the mailbox at the front of Freely Lakes.

"Wow, it looks like somebody's birthday party." Charlotte laughed. "I guess that they're into the festive way of doing things."

"I guess." Ally took a deep breath and reminded herself of how important this was to her grandmother. She tried to have a good attitude, but her first instinct was that no place was good enough for her grandmother. She parked and glanced over at Charlotte. "We don't even have to go in you know. You don't have to do this."

Charlotte reached over and patted Ally's hand. "I'm not leaving you, sweetheart, you know that, don't you?" She met Ally's eyes. The two shared the same shade of green eyes, as did Ally's late mother.

"I'm just worried about you, Mee-Maw. What if something happens?"

"I'm only a few minutes away from where you will be. If I need you, I can call you."

Ally nodded. She turned the car off. "I guess since moving back home it's been so nice to have you there when I wake up in the morning again."

"I appreciate that, Ally, but maybe it's not me that makes the difference. Maybe you're just longing to have someone there when you wake up again. Divorce is hard, sweetheart." She smiled gently.

Ally grimaced. "You could be right about that. I didn't really think about living alone again when I was going through the divorce."

"Give it time, you're going to find that you love having some room to expand. It's part of the healing process to get to know yourself again."

"How did you get so wise, Mee-Maw?"

"I raised your mother, and you. I spent decades figuring life out, and starting all over again, many times. Just like I am now. I used to be afraid of change, now I'm just excited. It's never as bad as you expect, and there are always surprises just around the corner."

“I hope you’re right.” Ally opened the door of the car and stepped out. Her grandmother did as well. As they walked across the parking lot Ally noticed that there were several cars parked near the entrance of the building. Many of them had handicapped placards, some did not. She didn’t like to think of her grandmother as getting older, maybe that was another reason why she didn’t like the idea of Charlotte moving into a retirement community. As they walked towards the building Ally noticed a man in a suit. He stood by the door.

“Hello there.” As they walked up, the man took off his hat, and dipped his head respectfully. “Welcome to Freely Lakes Retirement Community.”

“Why, thank you.” Charlotte smiled. “What a lovely greeting.”

“Are you here for the open house?” He held the door open for them.

“Yes, we are. I’m planning to move in.” Charlotte pushed a few strands of her long, gray hair back behind one ear. “Perhaps you could give us a tour?"

"Ah, I would enjoy nothing more, my lady, but alas my role is only as a lowly doorman today. I'm sure there is someone inside who will be more than happy to assist you." He bowed his head again. Charlotte giggled. Ally's eyes widened as she followed behind her grandmother.

"Did you really just giggle?"

"I did." Charlotte grinned. "I love the way he talked to me."

"Oh boy, I see that I'm going to have to keep an eye on you."

"We will look out for each other." Charlotte nodded. "Besides, I will need some way to keep myself busy while you and your detective get to know each other."

"Mee-Maw, nothing's happened!"

"Mm hm."

As they walked down the hall Charlotte pointed out the beautiful live plants that lined the walls. "You know how much I despise artificial flowers. Someone puts a lot of effort into caring for these plants. That's a good sign."

"They are nice." Ally opened the door to the recreation room. Inside were several folding tables and an assortment of food to select from. With so many options to choose from, Ally felt her stomach rumble. She hadn't taken any time to have breakfast that morning.

"Look, they have muffins." She made a quick turn to the food table.

"Go on, I'm going to introduce myself to a few people." Charlotte walked towards a group of women that stood around another table. Ally set down the boxes of chocolates they brought to share in order to pick up one of the muffins from the tray. As soon as she set them down she heard a high pitched squeal.

"Are those what I think they are?" A towering woman with white curls and a booming voice reached for the top box of chocolates.

"They're from Charlotte's Chocolate Heaven." Ally smiled, then took a bite of her muffin.

"Oh, that place is fabulous! I just love her chocolates. I never get over there anymore to get some myself, but my friends all know that they are my favorite. Do you think that anyone would notice if I took the whole box?"

Ally grinned. "No, I don't think so. I'm sure my grandmother would love to know that she has such a big fan. She's planning to move in here soon."

"Oh, I know. It will be amazing! I will have to become best friends with her. Just promise me that you won't tell her that it's because of the chocolates."

Ally couldn't help but grin at the woman's enthusiasm. "I promise. Hurry and take those to your room before someone catches you."

"I will!" She winked and hurried off. Charlotte walked up behind Ally.

"One box is already gone? Oh dear, I guess we should have brought more."

"Next time we will." Ally grinned.

"Shall we take a walk along the lake?" Charlotte offered Ally her arm. "Someone just told me there is a family of ducks that I would like to see for myself."

"Absolutely."

The two women made their way down a long, winding path that led to a small, peaceful lake. "I hate to admit it, but this place is beautiful," Ally said.

"And I don't have to lift a finger. Someone else mows the lawn, someone else waters the garden. I just get to enjoy it. What could be better than that?"

"But won't you miss Arnold?"

"Of course. But I will get to visit him all the time. Besides, he has Peaches to keep him company."

"I'm not so sure he likes that idea." Ally laughed. Her laughter carried across the calm water of the lake. She took a deep breath of the fresh air. She really could see why her grandmother would want to live at Freely Lakes. The people were nice, the setting was idyllic, and the sense of freedom was distinctly in the air.

"I guess we'll have to pick out your apartment."

"Oh, I already did! There are a few apartments that overlook the lake. I'd really like one of those. Unfortunately, they're all occupied at the moment, but the manager assured me that she will work on it for me. I'm willing to live in a different one until one of those becomes available."

"What if we offer someone who lives in one of the apartments free chocolates for life if they switch with you?" Ally laughed.

"Good idea. But one thing I've learned in life, Ally, is that patience will get you everything. I have plenty of time to look forward to the room. Sometimes the anticipation is just as sweet."

"I wish I had your patience." Ally sighed. "Sometimes it feels like all I do is try to force the hand of fate, and it never works."

"How can you say that?" Charlotte looked over at her with a small smile. "You're here with me, aren't you?"

"Good point." Ally grinned.

As they walked back towards the main building, Ally noticed the woman who had taken the entire box of chocolates. She walked with an unsteady gait.

"Oh dear, that's Myrtle Dents, isn't it?" Charlotte clucked her tongue. "Someone got into the sauce far too early."

"Do you know her well?"

"Not very. Her family has lived in Freely for a long time. In fact I spoke to her earlier this week when I stopped in. She lives in one of the rooms that overlook the lake, and offered to show me the view. Of course, she was sober then." Charlotte shook her head as the woman swayed back and forth along the path. "Retirement is no excuse for picking up bad habits. Hopefully she doesn't drive."

"Now, Mee-Maw, we can't judge. I saw her not that long ago when she took some chocolates we brought with and she was sharp as a tack. Maybe she's on some kind of medication that makes her a bit loopy."

"Maybe. But I've seen a lot of drunk people in my time, and that woman looks drunk to me."

"I guess we won't know unless we ask." Ally started to walk towards the woman, but before she could reach her another woman took Myrtle's arm and led her away. Ally thought that the woman looked familiar, but she had met a lot of new people at the open house and wasn't quite sure where she had seen her.

"Let's head back inside, I think they are going to do a little presentation about the different activities that are available at the center."

"Great." Ally nodded. She stared after Myrtle for a moment, then followed her grandmother back to the main building. Inside they had set up an area with mockups representing all of the different activities that residents could choose from. One of the women held a tennis racket to represent the tennis courts. She wore a cute, little, white tennis skirt.

"As you can see we have a variety of activities available to not only keep you on your toes, but give everyone the chance to socialize and get to know one another."

"Who would want to get to know that wench?" A slurred voice called out from the back of the room. Ally turned to see Myrtle leaning heavily on another woman's arm. She pointed at the woman with the tennis racket. "Ruth couldn't play tennis to save her life. Could you, Ruth? She just likes to wear the little skirts."

"Hush! You're making a scene, Myrtle. Stop acting so foolish!" Ruth said.

"I'm foolish? You're the one spreading rumors about me everywhere! I'm dying, huh? Well, guess what? I'm still here, aren't I?" She stomped her foot and nearly fell over. The woman beside her steadied her.

"Myrtle, stop this now, you're just tired." The

woman beside her said.

"I'm not tired. I'm healthy as a horse. Which is more than I can say for this one! She has a problem with popping pills, don't you, Ruth?"

"You shut your mouth!" Ruth swung the tennis racket so hard that Ally jumped back. She expected the racket to go flying, but Ruth kept her grip on it. She fixed Myrtle with such an angry glare that Ally thought the two might get into a fist fight.

"Okay, that's enough, ladies." The man who had opened the door for them moved between the two. "Why don't we put on some music?" He raised an eyebrow to another man who stood beside a radio. That man turned on music. Myrtle was led away by the woman at her side. The gentleman who had intervened offered his hand to Charlotte. "I wouldn't want you to get the wrong impression. We also have many social events, such as ballroom dancing. Would you like to join me?"

Charlotte grinned. "I certainly would." She

took his hand and cast a wink over her shoulder to Ally. Ally smiled, but her mind was still on the two women. If there was that much animosity between residents was it really the best place for her grandmother to live?

Ruth walked over to a table and sat down. She looked furious as she took a sip of her sugar-free soda.

Ally decided to see if she could gain any insight from the other residents. While her grandmother danced she sat down at a table with a small group of women.

"Wow! That was some argument. Does Myrtle often get drunk?" Ally asked casually.

"Myrtle?" A tiny woman on the other side of the table giggled. "No, never. She protested to having wine at the New Year's Eve party, said it wasn't fair to those who were on medications that shouldn't be mixed with alcohol."

"I guess she's changed her mind about that." The woman beside her said.

"Oh please, you know that Ruth had it coming." The tiny woman said. "Ruth thinks she's the belle of the ball because she is barely old enough to live here. She's determined to get one of the apartments that overlook the lake, and has decided that because Myrtle is one of the oldest residents that has a room with a view, she will be the next one to die. The cruel creature has even started to take bets as to how much longer Myrtle has. Who could ever think that was acceptable behavior?"

"Oh now, that's just her personality. She doesn't mean anything by it." The woman beside her shook her head. "I'm sure that if the two just spent some time together they would come to an understanding."

"Ethel, not everyone is a peacemaker like you." The smaller woman sighed. "No. I think if the two of them were in a room together that racket would be used for something other than tennis."

"Beth! You shouldn't say things like that!"

Ethel scowled. "You know how easily someone's reputation can get ruined by a rumor."

The third woman, who had been silent the entire time raised her hands into the air. "Ladies, drop it. This woman doesn't want to hear our dirty laundry. The truth is Freely Lakes is like a little town unto itself, it has its villains and its saints, and more than its share of drama. Too many old bitties watching daytime soap operas and trying to make it their reality."

"I am not an old bitty!" Beth lifted her chin.

"Neither am I." Ethel frowned.

"Well, I am." The woman stood up from her chair. "And I prefer it that way. I keep to myself, I read my books, I take my walks, and no one threatens me with a tennis racket. Maybe the two of you should stop worrying so much about Ruth and Myrtle and pay more attention to how you're spending your time. You could have knitted an entire sweater in the time it took you to gossip."

"Now, who's being dramatic?" Ethel rolled her eyes. Ally was a bit amused and slightly concerned by what she had heard. Freely Lakes sounded more like high school than a retirement home. The conversation ended when Charlotte was escorted to the table by her dance partner.

"Ally, this is Steven." She patted the man's shoulder. "Steven, this is my beautiful granddaughter, Ally."

Ally eyed Steven with some skepticism. "Nice to meet you, Steven. I was just learning about the ins and outs of Freely Lakes."

"Oh dear, I hope you didn't hear only one side." Steven chuckled. "We have our issues, just like any other place, but Freely Lakes is a safe and wonderful environment. I'm really looking forward to Charlotte joining us here."

"Me too." Charlotte smiled. "Ally, are you about ready to go? I want an early start tomorrow as I have a cake I would like to prepare at the shop. I think that it will be a perfect treat to have at a moving party. Don't you?"

"Sure." Ally stood up. She wrapped an arm around her grandmother's shoulders. There was something about Freely Lakes that made her feel very protective of Charlotte. "We should be going."

"I'll walk you out." Steven flashed another smile at Ally. Ally mustered a smile in return, but there wasn't much genuine feeling in it. As soon as she was alone with her grandmother in the car Ally turned to face her.

"I don't know about this place."

"What? Why?"

"Because, the people don't seem to get along. I mean, a fist fight almost broke out between two of the women there."

"Ally, that's a bit of an exaggeration. There are always going to be people who don't like each other. It's not a big deal."

"What if it's dangerous there?" Ally started the car and looked up at the building. "You can't tell what a place is really like just by visiting."

"Listen, Ally it's not as if I'm going to be locked away in a prison. If I move in and things don't work out then I am free to leave at any time. All right?" She reached out and patted Ally's hand. "I think it's sweet that you're so worried, but I really don't think that there is anything to be worried about. I've never heard any bad things about this place. Now, how about that Steven?"

Ally couldn't help but smile as her grandmother chattered about Steven for the entire car ride. Maybe she was being overprotective and suspicious. Her grandmother was a strong and vibrant woman who could take care of herself.

Chapter Three

The next day Ally arrived at the shop early. She wanted to have another shot at the smudged window. She thought she had her grandmother beat to the shop, but to her surprise she was greeted by the sound of a mixer.

"Mee-Maw?"

"I'm here." Charlotte stepped out from the back room. "I'm sorry, Ally, I came in early because I want to get this recipe just right, I've made some tweaks to it. I want to wow my new neighbors with my amazing decadent chocolate cake. Would you like to help me with it?"

"Sure. I was just going to clean the front window first."

"All right, that's fine, I have to start over anyway because I added too much coffee." She sighed and rolled her eyes. "There's always something."

"I'll be right there." Ally smiled. She knew that

when her grandmother tried out new cake recipes or adjusted old ones it meant a lot of delicious mistake-cakes for her to sample. As she was gathering the items she would need for cleaning she heard the bell over the unlocked door. She looked up to see three regulars walk in. The three women were not only frequent customers, but an unending source of gossip. Mrs. White dabbed at her eyes with a tissue as she stepped inside.

"Mrs. White, is something wrong?" Ally frowned. "We're not actually open yet."

"Oh please, I need some chocolate to make this better." Mrs. White wiped her eyes again. Mrs. Cale patted her shoulder.

"There there, dear one."

Ally thought about her options for a moment. She was the manager and regular customers were in dire need of comfort food.

"I'll find something I can put out." Ally took out a tray of chocolates from the refrigerated display cabinet and placed it on the counter.

"Can you believe that she's gone?" Mrs. Bing shook her head.

"Who's gone?" Ally paused behind the counter and looked at the three women.

"Myrtle Dents. They found her this morning on the floor of her room at Freely Lakes."

"What?" Ally gasped. "But we just saw her yesterday. Mee-Maw and I went there for the open house."

"It happens fast when it happens." Mrs. White shook her head.

"Ally, what's going on?" Charlotte stuck her head out from the back room. "I thought you were going to help me with the cake. Oh, I didn't realize that we had customers." She smiled at the three women.

"Mee-Maw, I have some bad news." Ally frowned.

"What is it?" Charlotte stepped all the way out from the back room.

"Myrtle, the woman we saw yesterday, passed

away this morning."

"Oh no!" Just as Charlotte rounded the counter, the door to the shop swung open. Mrs. Cale raised a nut cluster to her mouth and was about to chomp down on it. Luke Elm bolted through the door and ran right up to Mrs. Cale. He slapped the chocolate out of her hand before she could put it into her mouth.

"Luke!" Ally gasped as she watched the chocolate bounce across the floor.

"What are you doing?" Mrs. Cale demanded and grasped her purse as if she might take a swing at him. Ally ducked between them before she could.

"No one eat any chocolates! Or anything else made in this shop!" Luke looked over at Ally and then at Charlotte. He then turned to the three customers. "Ladies, if you'll please leave the shop I need to discuss some things with the owner."

"No more chocolates?" Mrs. Cale's chin trembled. "But, but..."

"Mrs. Cale, listen to the detective. I'll make sure you and the others each get your own box of chocolates for free." Charlotte settled her gaze on Luke with such heat that Ally winced. She knew that look from many years of experience.

"All right." Mrs. Cale nodded. She and the other two women made their way past Luke just as several police officers flooded into the shop after them.

"Ally, I need to speak to you," Luke said.

"Why? What is going on here?" Ally looked at the officers that began to pick up different items around the shop.

"We tested the chocolates that Myrtle ate. The ones from this shop. They tested positive for antifreeze."

"What?" Ally grabbed the counter to hold herself up. "That's not possible."

"I don't know how it happened, Ally, but it's true. I saw the test myself. I insisted on it."

Ally stared at him and slowly shook her head.

"Then test it again, and again."

"Ally, there's no point. I was there for the testing. The chocolates were in a box from this shop. Myrtle didn't die of natural causes, she was poisoned. We have to shut the shop down just in case there are any more poisoned chocolates here."

"You're shutting us down?" Charlotte scowled at him. "Luke, you should know better. Of course none of our chocolates are poisoned."

"Actually, some of them are." He frowned, but his tone remained respectful. "Now, I don't believe that you and Ally would have anything to do with that, but somehow those chocolates ended up filled with antifreeze, and now a woman is dead." He plucked a napkin from the counter and leaned down to pick up the nut cluster that Mrs. Cale had almost eaten. "We don't want two deaths on our hands, do we?"

"Well, I never..." Charlotte started to respond, but she was interrupted by another voice.

"Detective." One of the officers stuck his head

in from the back room. He held up a bottle of antifreeze. "Found it on the back step."

"It's for the van!" Ally's heart began to race. "I bought it for the van!"

"Log it into evidence." Luke nodded.

"Are you going to arrest us?" Ally looked over at her grandmother. "Just take me okay, Luke?"

"Wait a minute." Luke rested his hands on the curve of her shoulders and looked into her eyes. "Try to relax, I'm not arresting anyone. We're here to make sure that you and Charlotte are safe just as much as we are here to make sure the rest of the town is. No one is being accused of a crime, right now we are just trying to gather evidence and figure out what happened here and make sure no one else gets hurt."

"This is unreal." Ally shook her head and started to pull away from him, but his hands tightened on her shoulders.

"Ally, look at me."

Ally met his eyes as anxiety boiled within her.

"Luke, I..."

"It's okay. Just calm down. We're going to figure this out. All right? You have to trust me."

Ally pursed her lips. She wasn't sure how she could calm down while police officers were combing through everything in the shop. Charlotte snatched up a wooden cat before it could fall off a shelf.

"Please be careful." She frowned at the officer who bumped into it. The shop was full of handmade pieces of art that Charlotte had collected over the years.

"Sorry, Ma'am."

Ally pulled away from Luke and walked over to her grandmother. She wrapped her arm around her. "Maybe we should go outside while they do the search."

"No, absolutely not." Charlotte glared at the officers. "I will be right here, watching everything they do and exactly who does it. I have never been so offended."

"Mee-Maw, what can they do? They found poison in the chocolates. They have to investigate."

Charlotte looked straight over at Luke. "Maybe they should be investigating how the chocolates were poisoned after they left the shop, because it certainly didn't happen here. Instead of wasting time on believing that there is something to find in the shop, the focus should be on who had a reason to bring harm to Myrtle."

"I can assure you, Charlotte, we are looking into all leads. However, we can't allow the public to be at risk. Once we ensure that the shop is safe, it will be reopened and you two can conduct business as usual."

"Except that everyone in town will know that it was searched by police and connected with a murder." Charlotte crossed her arms. Ally placed a hand on her grandmother's arm.

"We can't blame Luke, Mee-Maw."

"Can't we?"

"Charlotte please, I'm only doing my job here."

"And I'm only trying to protect my business and my reputation," Charlotte stated.

Ally frowned. She understood why Luke was there. A woman was dead, and all of the evidence so far pointed right to the shop. But she felt that the way he handled the situation could have been much more delicate and less public. But maybe she was being oversensitive.

"How long will this take?" Ally met his eyes.

"It shouldn't take too long. They'll take the paperwork away to look at. They'll have to get rid of all of the open consumables in the shop. They'll also have to test some samples of the chocolates that you have here, some of the raw ingredients and inspect some of your equipment, and then wait for the health department to clear the shop."

"This is ridiculous." Charlotte shook her head sharply. "And who is investigating where the real crime actually occurred?"

"I understand why you are upset, Charlotte, but I..."

"It's Mrs. Sweet to you." Charlotte raised an eyebrow. Luke lowered his eyes. He glanced over at Ally who avoided looking back at him.

"Yes, Mrs. Sweet. I understand why you are upset, but the fact remains that a woman is dead and the chocolates she ate were from your shop. They were laced with antifreeze."

"Oh no, she wasn't drunk yesterday!" The words spilled from Charlotte's lips before she could stop them.

"So, you admit to having contact with Myrtle yesterday?" Luke pulled out his notepad.

"Admit? As if I'm confessing something? Yes, we saw her yesterday," Charlotte said.

Ally's heart sunk as she realized that Myrtle didn't start acting strange until after she took one of the boxes of chocolates from Ally. As she liked the chocolates so much, Myrtle had likely eaten quite a bit of the box.

"Ally, did you notice anything that I should know about?" Luke tried to meet her eyes.

"I don't know," Ally whispered.

"Not now, Ally. They're headed to the kitchen. I'm going with them." Charlotte followed the majority of the officers into the kitchen.

"Ally?" Luke reached a hand out to stop her from moving past the counter to follow her grandmother. "Anything you have to tell me could only help."

"I don't know about that." Ally tried not to be swayed by the warmth in his eyes.

"I don't think you had anything to do with this, Ally. Anything you can tell me will only make things easier."

"Let me think about it." Ally gently grasped his forearm and swept it out of her way so that she could join her grandmother in the kitchen. She could feel Luke's eyes still on her until the door swung closed behind her. Ally and Charlotte were silent as they observed the officers finishing their search. Several chocolates were bagged as evidence. The partly-made batter for Charlotte's chocolate cake that she was in the middle of baking was confiscated. Any open ingredients were bagged. Ally held her grandmother's hand. She could feel it tremble.

"Never in my life," Charlotte whispered as she shook her head. Ally squeezed her hand.

Once the officers filed out of the shop, one remained to tape a piece of paper onto the front window. "This may not be removed by anyone, but the health department or a police officer." He looked at each woman with warning. Ally only nodded. Charlotte didn't respond at all. After he left, Ally stared out through the window at the sign that was affixed to the glass. Not only was it overwhelming to think that somehow their chocolates were connected to the death of a woman, it was embarrassing to think that the entire community would be aware of the supposed connection.

"Oh, Mee-Maw, what are we going to do?"

Ally's breath caught in her chest. In her mind everything was about to fall apart. They would lose the shop, the cottage, and then what? Could they even end up in prison?

"Let's see, your young detective..."

"He's not my young detective."

Charlotte took a deep breath and smacked her palms together a few times.

"Okay, young Luke has shut down the shop because a woman died from eating poisoned chocolates. Chocolates that appear to have come from our shop."

"What do you mean?"

"Well Ally, did you happen to mix some antifreeze in when you made them?"

"Mee-Maw!"

"Then we have nothing to worry about, do we?" Charlotte smiled, but her expression was strained. "All we need to do is figure out who did put the antifreeze in the chocolates, then we will be able to open back up and Myrtle's murder will be solved. It's simple really. If we get caught up in things that we can't control then we'll never get out of this situation. In fact, Ally, I'm going to ask you to do something that I normally wouldn't."

"What's that?" Ally looked at her grandmother curiously. She had always known her to be clever, but the glint in her eyes was more intense than usual.

"I want you to see if you can get information from Luke. I want proof that those chocolates came from our shop. I want to know what he saw when he found the chocolates, how many she ate, basically all of the details."

"What makes you think he'll tell me any of that?"

"The way he looks at you, Ally. There's no question in my mind that if you ask, he's going to answer." Ally rolled her eyes and shook her head.

"You've got it wrong, Mee-Maw. Luke is too by the book to reveal anything he shouldn't."

"Well, then at most you'll waste a little time.

Right?"

"I guess." Ally nodded. She took a deep breath. "You're right. There's no point in sitting around and waiting for Luke to come back with an arrest warrant."

"Ally, don't think like that. We haven't done anything wrong. It's a mistake, a terrible mistake, but a mistake just the same."

"I don't know if I can really consider it a mistake. Even though I know that Luke didn't have control over this, it still bothers me. He knows us, he knows that we didn't do it."

"Does he? I mean, we haven't known him that long. He could very well have some doubts. Besides, even if he is certain that we had nothing to do with it, he still has a job to do. Just go and talk to him. Let's find out for sure what he knows before we look into things ourselves a bit."

"I doubt that he'll like that," Ally said.

"Just like he has a job to do, so do we! Ally, we're going to get to the bottom of this, and get our names cleared and the shop back open."

"Absolutely!"

Chapter Four

Ally left the shop and headed back to the cottage. She wanted to take a few minutes to clear her head before talking to Luke. The best way to do that was to share her thoughts with Peaches. The cat was the best listener that she knew. When she opened the door to the cottage she heard a screech and a snort. A sigh rippled through her. It was going to take longer than she had thought for the new housemates to get along. Arnold was spending more time in the house than he used to. He was probably enjoying spending time hassling Peaches.

"Peaches, come here, sweetie." Ally clucked her tongue to call the cat. Peaches bounded down the hall and followed Ally into her bedroom. Ally closed the door to give Peaches a break from Arnold. She sat down on her bed. The cat jumped right up beside her.

"I'm in quite a mess, Peaches. I don't understand how the chocolates could have been poisoned. I made them, I packaged them, I even hand-delivered them. So, how could the poison get inside them?" She groaned and flopped back on the bed. "Now, Mee-Maw wants me to try and get Luke to share the evidence he found with me. I don't know if he will be as responsive to me as she thinks he will be."

Peaches pranced right up onto Ally's stomach and curled up. She stretched out her paws and yawned. "Oh, am I boring you?" Ally scratched her ears. "Maybe you're right. Maybe I'm over thinking it. Luke is a reasonable man, from what I know of him." She bit into her bottom lip as she recalled the tension that had built up between her and Luke. She did her best to avoid him as she wasn't sure what to make of how she felt when she was around him. With her divorce still fresh in her mind, and adjusting to being back in the town she grew up in, she had enough confusing emotions to deal with. The strange thing was that when she was around Luke, all of that confusion disappeared. "Then again, what if he does listen?

What if he will tell me what I need to know? You're right, Peaches, it's worth a try."

She pulled herself up off the bed and walked towards the closet. She wanted to find out what she could from Luke. Ally looked through her closet for something to wear. She mostly wore jeans and a flannelette top since moving back to Blue River, but she wanted to wear something a bit smarter to give her the confidence to talk to Luke about the case. She chose a blouse and a snug wraparound skirt. Even as she smoothed it down over her hips her heart fluttered with guilt that she was going to ask Luke to reveal information to her. But desperate times called for desperate measures, at least that's what she told herself. With one more look in the mirror she smoothed her hair down. Now, she had to hope that Luke really did like her and would want to share the information with her.

***

When Ally arrived at the police station she was greeted by a woman with short, gray hair and thick, blue glasses.

"What is it that you want?" She squinted at Ally.

"I need to speak with Luke, please."

"And you are?"

"Uh, a friend."

"Are you aware that this is a place of work? I mean, you can't just walk in and ask to talk to your buddy." She raised a pencil thin, gray eyebrow. "Not only that, it is a police station. Your friend Luke has a job to do, and I'm sure he's doing it."

"Ally?" Luke walked out of the back room and towards the front desk. "What are you doing here?"

"Your friend is here to see you." The woman rolled her eyes and shifted her chair away from the desk.

Luke's lips quirked slightly as if he might smile, but he caught himself before he did, and pressed his lips together hard.

"What can I help you with, Ally?" Luke said as

he gestured for her to walk away from the woman at the front desk so they were out of earshot.

"It's more about what you can do for me, Luke." Ally did her best to offer a sweet smile. She wasn't sure if it was effective, but Luke's eyes did appear to light up.

"Anything you need." He rested one hand on the wall beside him.

"I want you to open the shop."

"Anything, but that." He grimaced.

"Surely, you can make an exception." Ally tossed her hair over her shoulder. Or at least she attempted to. She only managed to scratch the side of her neck and get one of her rings tangled. She jerked her hand free and bit her tongue to keep from crying out. Luke quirked a brow. He lowered his hand from the wall and met her eyes.

"Are you asking me for a personal favor, Ally?"

"Would that work?"

"Come with me." He held open the partition

to the rest of the station. Ally's heart skipped a beat. She wasn't sure if it was a good idea to willingly cross that line. What would be next? Would he fingerprint her? Take her mugshot? She shuddered at the thought.

"Why don't we talk outside?" Ally asked.

"I'd like to talk to you at my desk." He gestured towards another area of the open room.

"Why?"

"Look Ally, I know you're probably upset, but until we can ensure the safety of the public the shop has to stay closed."

"Fine, don't open it. There's something else you can do for me."

"What is it?" He met her eyes. Ally was quite aware that the woman was still watching her.

"I want to see what evidence you have against the shop."

"Huh?" He took a slight step back. "What do you mean see it?"

"I mean, you came into the shop, you invaded

it with a bunch of police officers, and shut it down. But never once did you show us what proof you had that gave you the right to do so."

"Ally, I don't have to show you proof. I had a warrant to search the shop, which your grandmother was served. I also had the go ahead from the health department to shutter the shop until the matter could be cleared up."

"Okay fine, but that's just paperwork." Ally crossed her arms. "That doesn't amount to much to me."

"So, you're asking to see what evidence I used to get the warrant?" He raked his gaze along her face. Ally did her best to keep every twitch under control. She didn't want Luke to think that she would back down for any reason. But the truth was she was horrified by the idea of paperwork being sent to a judge that included an accusation that somehow she or her grandmother had poisoned Myrtle. Her stomach churned with the very thought of that accusation lingering as a permanent smudge on her grandmother's reputation.

"Yes, if you're going to investigate us, then I would like to know on what grounds."

"Ally, you know it isn't like that." He moved past the partition between the lobby and the rest of the police station. The closer he got to her the more Ally's determination faded. She wanted to be angry, but his presence soothed her nerves. There was no explanation for it, that's just how it was.

"Do I? Because it seems just like that. If you really believe that we had nothing to do with the crime then it shouldn't be a problem to show me what evidence you have. I want to know if the chocolates that poisoned Myrtle were really ours."

"They were in a box from your shop."

"That doesn't mean that they weren't tampered with afterwards."

"How do you think someone would tamper with chocolates?" He shook his head. "I don't think that's possible."

"It must have been, because I packaged those chocolates myself. No one else besides Charlotte and me could have touched them. Something must have happened to them after they were already at the facility."

"That sounds like something to discuss. So please, join me at my desk." He rested one hand on her shoulder. His touch was light and in no way restraining, but Ally's entire body tensed in reaction to it.

"I don't see why we can't talk outside."

"And I don't see why we can't talk at my desk. Ally, you are involved in a criminal case, and it's best if we speak somewhere a bit more structured. If you can't work with me on this, I'm not sure how we're going to get anywhere."

Ally eyed him for a moment. For some odd reason she felt as if he was referring to more than just the case.

"All right." She nodded. "But I am free to leave at any time?"

“Of course you are.” He removed his hand from her shoulder and held the partition open again. This time Ally walked through it. As they made their way towards his desk Ally caught sight of a poster on the wall that promoted the upcoming blood drive. The sharp point of the needle on the poster made an idea pop into her head.

“Wait a minute. Could someone have injected the poison into the chocolates? That would barely leave a mark.”

“I don’t know. I guess it’s possible. But we might not have a way to prove it. It’s worth looking into though, but if the chocolates melted even a little the hole would disappear.”

“That doesn’t mean it didn’t happen.”

“No, of course it doesn’t, but it’s nothing we can use to reopen the shop. We need to find out what happened to those chocolates beyond a shadow of a doubt.”

“Okay, then tell me what evidence you have.”

Luke pulled out a chair and looked at Ally. "First, you tell me what you know."

"What I know?"

Luke patted the top of the chair. "Have a seat."

Ally narrowed her eyes. "I came here to find out information from you, not be questioned."

"And I need to question you for the case. So, we both need something the other can provide. You answer my questions, I'll answer yours." He smiled.

"You first."

"I'm afraid that's not how it works. If you would please sit down." He patted the back of the chair again. Ally eased herself into the chair. Luke sat down behind his desk and settled his gaze on her. "Did you see Myrtle eat the chocolates?"

Ally pursed her lips. She didn't think it would do anything to help her or her grandmother's case if she told him that she had seen Myrtle take an entire box of chocolates, not long before the woman could barely stand upright.

"Not exactly."

"Not exactly?" Luke sighed and ran his hands down his cheeks. "Okay so, you want me to share my information with you, but you're not willing to share your information with me. How is that going to work?"

"My information isn't going to land you in jail."

"Ally." Luke leaned forward. His voice lowered as he looked directly into her eyes. "Unless I believe that you are somehow responsible for Myrtle's death, which I don't, I am not going to arrest you."

"And my grandmother?"

"I don't think they make cuffs that could hold her." Luke cracked a smile.

"I don't think it's funny." Ally crossed her arms, but she smiled slightly.

"You can't really believe that I suspect you or Charlotte."

"I know that the shop is closed."

"What if it wasn't? Either way the chocolates that were poisoned came from your shop, there's no getting around that. How would it look if I didn't close down the shop? I have people I answer to, and they would want an explanation from me about not following the proper procedures."

"I see." Ally felt some relief that maybe Luke wasn't focused on them as suspects. "Well, I do know that Myrtle was a big fan of my grandmother's chocolates. When she saw the boxes of chocolates on the table she asked me if she could take one of the boxes. I agreed, and she took an entire box of chocolates."

"Wow. It seems like she ate most of them."

"But there is no way that they were poisoned at the time she took them. No one else besides me and Charlotte had touched them or been near them. Now, I gave you some information, it's your turn to give me some. I want the photographic evidence. Maybe if I look at the photos I can help."

Luke studied her for a moment. "Okay, I'll

show what I can in case there's something in them that you notice that can help me solve the case. I believe that I can trust you with this information. Can I?"

The question took Ally by surprise. She had been focused only on whether she could trust him, not the other way around.

"Yes." She held his gaze. He tapped his fingertips against a folder on his desk and he moved it between them. Ally braced herself for what she was about to see.

"In here are a few photographs of the crime scene," Luke said.

Luke flipped it open. Inside were three large photographs. The first was of a police outline where the body had been found. It was on the plush carpet beside the bed. There was no photograph of the body, which Ally was grateful for. Luke showed her the next photograph. This one was of the bedside table. On the table Ally could see that there was an open box of chocolates, a deck of cards, a business card of some kind, and a greeting card. She couldn't make out the writing on the chocolate box or what the business card or greeting card said.

The last photograph was a close up of the box of chocolates on Myrtle's bedside table. A box of chocolates, from Charlotte's Chocolate Heaven. Ally was stunned as she stared at the box. She was certain that she would be able to prove to Luke that there was some mistake, but the name of the shop was printed on the box. There were only three chocolates left in the box.

"Can you see anything that proves the chocolates didn't come from the shop?" Luke asked. Ally just shook her head. "Anything that indicates how they were poisoned?" Ally shook her head again. "Anything you want to tell me, Ally?"

"No," she managed to say.

"Why don't I make us a coffee and you can think about it?"

Ally nodded as Luke closed the folder and moved it to the corner of his desk. He walked to the back room to make coffee.

Ally wanted to look at the photos again. Maybe if she had more time to look at them or if she could show them to her grandmother she would be able to work out if something was out of place. Ally knew that Luke wouldn't give her a copy of the photographs. She could hear the coffee machine going. She looked around to make sure no one was watching and slowly slid the folder towards her. She pulled out her phone and snapped a picture of the photo that showed the box of chocolates. The moment she did she felt guilty because she knew that she had just broken his trust. But with the name of the chocolate shop on the side of the box, she wondered how long he would believe in her innocence. If the chocolates were from the shop, if they were poisoned with antifreeze, then all of the evidence pointed at her and her grandmother. She could only hope that the police would need more evidence than that to initiate an arrest. She heard footsteps coming back towards her.

She snapped the folder shut and moved it back to the corner of his desk where he had left it. A moment later he held out a cup of coffee to her.

"Think of anything important?"

"No." Ally took the coffee. He sat down across from her.

"I was hoping you might. I'm at a dead end so far."

Ally shook her head. "All I can tell you is that those chocolates were not poisoned when I made them, or when I picked them up from the shop."

"Wait a minute." Luke leaned forward and looked into her eyes. "Are you saying you left the chocolates at the shop overnight?"

"Well, yes. We picked them up in the morning to take with us to the open house."

"So anyone could have accessed them?"

"Not anyone. Only Mee-Maw and I have a key."

"But someone could have broken in?"

Ally started to shake her head, but then she recalled opening up the shop that morning. “There were smudges on the window I had cleaned the previous day and I had a difficult time unlocking the door that morning, but I thought it was just because I was tired.”

“I think that you need to consider that someone might have broken in and poisoned the chocolates.”

Ally grimaced. “But the boxes were sealed. They were still sealed when I picked them up.”

“Are you sure about that? Did you check them?”

Ally closed her eyes. “The morning was so hectic, we were running late. I don’t know for sure if I checked them.”

“Okay. That’s a place to start.” Luke reached across the desk and gave her hand a light stroke. “Don’t worry, all right? I’m on this. Everything will work out in the end.”

Ally’s hand tingled where he touched it. Her

heart flipped with the determination of his reassurance. She desperately wanted to believe him and his clear gaze, the soft curve of his lips, and the gentle pressure of his touch, all worked together to convince her that he might just be right.

Chapter Five

By the time Ally arrived back at the cottage, all the reassurance she had felt from Luke had disappeared. She was in full panic mode as she tried to figure out what could have happened.

"Ally? What did you find out?" Charlotte left the stove and what she was stirring. "Is Luke planning on making an arrest?"

"Not yet." Ally frowned. "I took a picture of one of the crime scene photos, it shows the box of chocolates. It didn't come out great, but here take a look." Ally handed her the phone. While her grandmother looked at the picture Ally paced throughout the kitchen. "It's not looking good, Mee-Maw. Luke thinks it's possible that someone broke in the night before the open house and poisoned thc chocolates."

"Luke is wrong."

"That's what I thought at first. But then I remembered that the window I had cleaned the day before was smudged and the lock was difficult to open."

"No, he's wrong about the entire thing."

"What do you mean?" Ally turned to face her grandmother.

"I mean that the chocolates in this photograph are not from our shop." She held up the picture with the three remaining chocolates in the box.

"But it says right on the side of the box..."

"I don't care what it says on the side of the box. I know my chocolates, and these are not them."

"How do you know?" Ally peered at the picture.

"Whoever made these walnut, expresso creams used a whole walnut and it's not caramelized, I only use half a caramelized walnut on these chocolates."

"Are you sure it's whole?" Ally raised an eyebrow. "The picture isn't that great."

"I'm sure. I know the difference," Charlotte said emphatically. "You have only made the expresso, walnut chocolates with me so there is no way you could have made that mistake. Could you?"

"No," Ally said.

"Those chocolates did not come from our shop! Something is definitely not adding up here."

"What we need to do is find out where those chocolates came from. Maybe if we get into her room we could find some evidence of what happened with the chocolates."

"Do you really think that's a good idea?" Charlotte quirked an eyebrow. "If we get caught..."

"If I get caught. I will be the one going in, Mee-Maw."

"I don't know." Charlotte frowned. "It seems risky to me."

"It's the only way we can get some idea of who did this to Myrtle. If we can figure out where those other chocolates came from, then we might be able to track down the person that poisoned them. It seems pretty obvious that whoever did it was attempting to frame our shop. They made sure the chocolates looked similar to ours and they packaged them in some of our packaging. So, they are clever, and intent on pinning the blame on us. If we just sit on our hands this is only going to get worse."

"No, of course not, I don't want us to do that. I just think we need to consider the consequences."

"I just won't get caught." Ally smiled a little.

"Ah, there's the boldness I remember." Charlotte laughed. "All right, I guess we don't have much choice. But if you're going to do this, I'm going to go with you, to be your getaway driver."

"Hmm, and you wonder where I got that boldness from?"

"Oh, it wasn't my fault! You got that from your mother!"

"And who did she get it from?"

Charlotte sighed. "I suppose I might have my moments."

Ally grinned. "All right, we'll wait until about midnight, then everyone should be asleep. No one will notice if I slip in for a quick peek."

"And what if someone does? What if Luke shows up?"

Ally raised an eyebrow. "Well, he did tell me that he wouldn't arrest me."

"I guess that's reassuring, but I don't think he expects you to break into Myrtle's room."

"We can't think about what might go wrong we just have to be as prepared as we can and go for it. In the meantime we need to get a list of suspects going. I remember that altercation between Ruth and Myrtle. The ladies at the table where I sat were quite eager to talk about their ongoing feud. They said that Ruth was even taking bets about when Myrtle would die."

"Atrocious. But that doesn't mean it's true or

that she did it."

"No, it doesn't, but it does give us a place to start," Ally said. "Was she married?"

"Divorced."

"What about kids, did Myrtle have any?"

"Two I think. A boy and a girl. But they moved away a long time ago."

"I'll have to check into that, too." Ally nodded.

"Let's just hope that we can figure out something fast enough to be able to get the shop back open before people forget we're even there."

"Oh, I don't think they will forget, but it would be nice if they forgot about this little mess we've gotten ourselves into," Ally said.

"Who knew that making delicious chocolates could lead to homicide?"

"I don't know, Mee-Maw, but until we figure all of this out you should be cautious of everyone at Freely Lakes. Anyone there could have been involved in this. As far as I am concerned everyone at Freely Lakes is a suspect."

"And as far as the police force and the community are concerned, so are we." Charlotte met her eyes. "We can't give them any more reason to suspect us."

"I'll be careful."

***

Peaches waited for Ally outside the bathroom door. Ally could hear her plaintive meowing. But for once she did not respond to it. She soaked in a warm bath and closed her eyes. Her nerves were on edge with the thought of breaking into Myrtle's room that night. She didn't exactly have the expertise to pull it off well. She would probably stuff it up and not even be able to get in. When she thought about it, her next thought was always Luke putting her in handcuffs. What was it about him that made her think he would stand by his word? After all she didn't know much about him, and in turn he didn't know that much about her. So what drove that connection that she felt for him every time she thought of him? It was hard to stay focused on the task at hand if her mind wandered incessantly to his hazel eyes and the subtle curve of his smile.

"Okay, out of the tub with you." Ally flicked the switch to drain the water and stepped out of the tub. She wrapped herself in a towel and walked out of the bathroom to look in her closet. Peaches swished her way around her ankles.

How did one dress for breaking and entering? She settled on a pair of black jeans and a black turtleneck. She wasn't sure why, but it seemed appropriate for the activity. She sat down on the edge of her bed to pull on her sneakers. The moment she did, Peaches jumped up into her lap. Ally smiled and pet her.

"Don't worry, darling, I'll be very careful." When she stood up Peaches jumped down. But she left behind a large amount of orange fur.

"Great. I look like a tiger." Ally laughed at how ridiculous the moment was. She brushed off the orange fur as best she could and then pulled her long, brown hair into a tight ponytail. Her stomach flipped. What if she got caught?

There was a soft knock on her door. “Ally?”

“Yes, Mee-Maw, it’s open.”

Charlotte opened the door and took in the sight of her granddaughter. “Well, don’t you look beautiful.”

“Beautiful?” Ally laughed.

“Black suits you.”

“Okay,” Ally said. “But the goal is for no one to see me.”

“Ally, I want you to know that you don’t have to do this. You are taking a big risk. What happens if you get caught? I don’t think I should let you do this.”

“Mee-Maw, I’m all grown up. I don’t have to have your permission.”

“Ha! That will never be true.” Charlotte’s eyes glimmered. “You will always be my little Ally.”

“Oh, Mee-Maw.”

“I mean it, Ally, if you’re caught this could cause you trouble for the rest of your life.”

"It will be fine, I promise." Ally hugged her. "Everyone will be sleeping. It will be just fine."

"If you say so." She cleared her throat. "I filled the gas tank and your car is ready to go. I also took Arnold out for his walk."

"Oh good." Ally smoothed her hair. "Then we should get going."

Charlotte nodded without a word. The two continued in silence as Charlotte drove Ally's car to Freely Lakes. Ally could see that most of the apartments in the building were dark. She was able to decipher which one was Myrtle's with her grandmother's directions. It was on the second floor, which would require Ally to do some climbing as she couldn't go through the front door to get in. Luckily, there was a fire escape that led right up to the window.

"Looks like I'll be in and out in no time." Ally smiled at her grandmother as she put on gloves.

"I hope so. I'll be waiting." Charlotte gripped the steering wheel tightly. "Be careful."

Ally stepped out of the car. She brushed a bit more of Peaches' orange fur off her pants. Then she moved towards the building. There was not a hint of movement anywhere on the property. It was clear that the residents of Freely Lakes were not night owls. When she reached the building she counted the windows to make sure that she hadn't lost track of the right room. She still had no idea what she was looking for exactly, but she hoped that she would be able to find something fast.

As quietly as Ally could she climbed the fire escape towards the window. Ally held her breath each time her shoe struck the metal rung of the steps. Once she was at the top she tried the window. A good part of her had expected that the window would be locked, she would never actually get into the room to conduct her search, and all would be right with the world. But that wasn't the case. The window slid open easily. Ally's heart began to race. She knew that the moment she swung her leg over that windowsill she would be committing a crime. She eased the screen out of the frame and set it down on the landing beside her. Then she peered into the dark room. There was no sign of anyone inside.

The door of the bedroom was closed. Ally took a deep breath and swung one leg over the windowsill, then the other. It occurred to her that Freely Lakes was not a very safe place at all, certainly not safe enough for her grandmother, if she could break in so easily. She pushed the thought out of her mind and made her way through the room in search of anything that would reveal where the chocolates had come from. She used a flashlight application on her phone to cast light throughout the room.

The first place she checked was the bedside table. As she had hoped the items she saw in the picture were still there, aside from the box of chocolates. She saw that the business card was for a lawyer. She snapped a picture of it. The greeting card was colorful, with a 'Just Because' message on the front. She opened it up and saw that it was addressed to Myrtle, but it just said 'Enjoy!' It wasn't signed by anyone. Ally set the greeting card back down and began to survey the room again.

In the trash can beside the bed she noticed that there was a red and white ribbon. She recognized it as a ribbon that they used on the boxes of chocolates they delivered, unless a different color was requested. So, the ribbon had come from the box of chocolates? Her mind spun as she recalled that she had tied the boxes of chocolates for the open house with green and gold ribbons. She suddenly recalled that the box of chocolates in the photo Luke had showed her had red not gold writing. The chocolates on the bedside table weren't the chocolates from the open house! So where were they?

Ally's mind focused in on finding the other box of chocolates. She looked under the bed, in the closet, and even in the dresser drawers. She wasn't paying much attention to the fact that she had been in the room for quite some time. Then she noticed the air vent. When she pointed her light in that direction, she saw a glimmer of gold.

Ally crouched down and popped open the air vent. She reached in and to her surprise there was the unopened box of chocolates. It had gold writing on it with green and gold ribbon just like the box of chocolates that Myrtle had taken on the day of the open house. Ally reached in and pulled it out. Just as she did, a bright light blinded her.

"Don't you move a muscle!"

Chapter Six

The thick voice was enough to make Ally's skin crawl with fear. She didn't dare to look in the man's direction. Her entire body ached with the desire to run and hide, but she knew better. There was no way that she could escape, the man was already towering over her. He slowly lowered his flashlight. As he did Ally could see that he wore a dark blue uniform. It looked similar to a police officer's, but it wasn't exactly the same.

"Who are you?" She stared up at him. His thick, black hair was a mass of curls and his dark blue eyes matched his uniform.

"I think you're the one that needs to answer the questions. The police are on their way. If you try to run, I will restrain you."

Ally could see from the way that his muscular frame strained against his uniform that he would have no problem with doing just that. "Please, this is all a mix up."

"Sure. You just fell into a crime scene? Did you trip on the way up the fire escape that you had no reason to be on?"

Ally bit into her bottom lip. The man's attitude made it quite clear that he was not interested in any explanations.

"I made a mistake, maybe you could just find a way to let this go?"

The sound of sirens tore through the quiet of Freely Lakes.

"That's not really for me to decide, sweetheart. I'm sure the cops will listen to your every word while you're being locked up." He shook his head. Then he pointed his light directly at her face again. "Ally Sweet?"

Ally's eyes widened. Not only had he caught her, but he now also knew her name, probably knew her. "Do I know you?"

"Wow. Ally Sweet." He shook his head. "I never would have predicted this. You're a long way from your pompoms."

Ally's cheeks heated up fast. She had one miserable year as a cheerleader in high school. It was something she very rarely divulged to anyone. The man before her must have known her from high school. But she didn't recognize him.

"I'm sorry, I don't know who you are."

"No, you wouldn't. You didn't then, and you have no reason to now." He lowered his flashlight again. "Up here, Detective!"

Ally groaned under her breath. Not only was she about to be arrested, but Luke would be the one who did it. It made sense that he would be the one who came to the invaded crime scene, since he was the lead detective on the case. She watched his dress shoe cross the windowsill, followed by the rest of him. When he saw her still crouched on the floor his face grew pale.

"Ally?"

Ally stood up slowly.

"Don't move." The man beside Luke warned.

"I'll take it from here, Jensen." Luke looked

over at the security guard. “Thanks for the alert.”

“Sure. It’s my job to keep the residents here safe. Mind if I use the door?”

“Go ahead, the room has already been contaminated.” Luke locked his eyes on Ally’s. Ally’s stomach twisted. As the security guard walked out of the room, Luke called down to the police officers below. “I’ve got this. Go on home.”

The officers didn’t argue. The lights and sirens were soon gone. Luke however, continued to stare right at Ally.

“What were you thinking?”

“Luke.”

“Wait, don’t. I don’t even know if I want you to speak to me. I don’t even know how I’m going to write this up. This is unbelievable. I told you I wouldn’t arrest you for the murder, did you think I wouldn’t arrest you for breaking and entering? For contaminating a crime scene?”

“You have to do what you have to do, Luke.”

“I didn’t tell you to talk, yet.” He ran his hands

back through his hair which Ally noticed had gotten a little longer. “What am I supposed to do about this, Ally? Jensen saw you here. I can’t just sweep this under the rug. You’re the prime suspect in a murder, and then I find you breaking into the victim’s apartment?”

Ally swallowed hard. She couldn’t think of a single way to defend herself. “The chocolates weren’t from our shop. I showed my grandmother the picture of them and…”

“Wait, what? Did you take the picture out of the folder?”

“No, I took a picture with my phone.”

“Ally! Wow.” He shook his head and turned his back to her. He didn’t seem concerned about her fleeing. “You told me that I could trust you.”

“I only showed her. And she could tell that they were not our chocolates. Someone is trying to frame us, Luke!”

Luke spun around to look at her. “Why would they have to do that?” He glowered. “You’re doing a fine job of it yourself." Ally lowered her eyes feeling remorseful.

"I just thought maybe I could find something to make all of this go away. And I did." Ally held up the box of chocolates. "I found these in the air vent. These were the chocolates I brought to the open house. They're not even opened."

"And that means absolutely nothing, Ally. Because you could have been planting them here when I caught you. There's no way to prove where those chocolates came from, because you compromised the crime scene. Your reckless choice has now forced my hand. There is no way to get out of this. I will have to reveal what happened here tonight to the prosecutor's office, and they will decide whether there is enough evidence to go ahead with an arrest warrant."

"You're going to arrest me?"

"It's the last thing I want to do, Ally, but I have no choice. You did this, not me. Now let's go."

"Are you going to handcuff me?"

"Not tonight. You'll have maybe a day before the prosecutor's office reviews the information. I suggest you use it to get a good lawyer."

***

When they reached the base of the stairs, Ally turned to look at Luke.

"I'm sorry."

"Me too." He shoved his hands into his pockets. "You should go. Did someone drive you here?" He sighed. "Let me guess. Mrs. Sweet?"

"I don't want her to get into any trouble."

"You shouldn't be getting into trouble either, Ally. I find it hard to believe that she thought this was okay for you to do."

"She didn't want me to."

"So, you just decided to risk everything?"

"I don't want her to lose the shop."

"If you had been patient, I could have figured all of this out. Don't you know that if you are innocent, which I believe you are, I am willing to fight for you?" Ally looked up at his words. She met his eyes. He held her gaze without the slightest attempt to look away from her. "I'll do whatever it takes, Ally. But there are rules that can't be bent or broken. Now, I'm in an awful position."

Ally was still stunned by his words. She sighed and held out the box of chocolates. "Can you do anything with these?"

"No, but I need to keep them," he said as he took them from her. "Like I said, they can't be considered evidence. But if you're right, and the chocolates were switched, then yes, someone really is trying to frame you, or your grandmother. I'll look into competitors or anyone that might have had something against the shop. In the meantime, promise me that you will not dig yourself any deeper into a jail cell, okay?"

Ally shivered at the thought. "I'll try."

"Ally?" She looked up at him. "Get a lawyer." He turned and walked away from her. As she watched him go a mixture of emotions plagued her. Part of her was intrigued by how determined he was to try and help her, another part was infuriated that he couldn't use his influence to protect her. As she walked back to the car the weight of the impending arrest warrant was almost too much for her.

"Ally? What's wrong? I heard the sirens."

Ally sunk down in the passenger seat. "It did not go well."

"What happened?"

"I was caught. Freely Lakes apparently has a great security guard." Her thoughts returned briefly to the man who had clearly recognized her. Jensen. The name didn't summon up any faces from her memory.

"But you weren't arrested?" Charlotte sighed with relief.

"No. Luke was there. Otherwise I probably would have been."

"Oh, good thing he was there! Maybe I shouldn't be so hard on him."

Ally tightened her lips. “Yes, good thing.” She stared out the window for the duration of the short drive back to the cottage.

***

Back at the cottage Ally stood by the dining room table.

“Look at this.” Ally showed Charlotte the crime scene photo of the box of chocolates again. “I don’t think that’s the box that I packaged the chocolates in, Mee-Maw. The boxes you gave me had gold not red writing.”

“Oh, you’re right.” Charlotte clicked her fingers.

“I found a box of chocolates in Myrtle’s room, but Luke took them from me. I think it’s the one that we took to the open house. I found it in the air vent. Obviously someone hid it there. The only question is, why would anyone hide it?”

“This is getting more confusing by the minute.” Charlotte frowned as she sat down at the table next to Ally. She looked up at her granddaughter. “Are you going to tell me what happened with Luke?”

“Nothing. He let me go.” She shrugged.

“Really?” Charlotte studied her. “Something tells me that there is more to it than that.”

“Mee-Maw, we can’t worry about that now. We have to focus on the chocolates. Look, we know now that the poisoned chocolates didn’t come from our shop. Someone else made the walnut, expresso creams, and those are the chocolates that were poisoned.”

“Right.” Charlotte nodded. “But who? And why? And how?”

“They aren’t very easy to make,” Ally said. “How would someone replicate the chocolates? Unless...”

“Unless what?” Charlotte asked.

“We had left over coffee cream in the fridge.”

“Do you think someone broke in and took it?”

“It’s possible.” Ally sat further forward. “Do you remember seeing it the morning after the murder?"

"No," Charlotte said. "But I wasn't looking out for it. It won't be there now anyway, the police would have taken it."

"So, that's probably how they made the chocolates."

"We still need to work out the who and why," Charlotte said.

"Myrtle had a business card on her bedside table for a lawyer. Maybe he'll have an idea of why someone would want her dead."

"Maybe."

"Did she have any other family?"

"Well, I can tell you this, Myrtle was worth a good amount of money. When her parents died, she was in her twenties, and her little sister, Stephanie, was still a minor. Her parents had left her everything in the will, on the condition that she would care for the younger girl. Which Myrtle did. She was the one we saw with Myrtle when she looked like she might fall down drunk. She recently moved from Freely to Blue River.

"What about her ex-husband?"

"Oh, they divorced a long time ago."

"Hm. He might still have a motive. Do you remember his name?"

"Nathan, or no, Nate. It was just Nate. I remember now. And the kids are Shirley and Mark."

"Do you think you could get hold of them, Mee-Maw?"

"Well, I imagine they'll be coming into town to deal with their mother's death."

"You're right!" Ally nodded. She glanced at her watch. It was well past one in the morning. "Tomorrow, we'll do our best to talk to all of them. And I'll call this lawyer." She didn't mention that she had two reasons for that. "I think we need to get as much information as we can tomorrow." Ally almost told her grandmother why, but she stopped herself. She didn't want Charlotte to worry.

"All right, good plan. Let's get some rest."

Ally nodded. Her grandmother went to her room to sleep. Ally did the same, but she couldn't even close her eyes. Peaches paced back and forth across her bed. She could sense Ally's unrest. Even with nuzzled cat kisses Ally couldn't calm down. Her mind filled with what it would be like to have to wear a jumpsuit, to be lumped in with criminals, to never find out exactly what her life could have been. She pulled Peaches close and snuggled her. What would it be like to never have her best friend around again? As she stared into the darkness of her room one question played through her mind on repeat. Would this be her last night as a free woman?

Chapter Seven

The next day the town buzzed with the arrival of Myrtle's family members, the closure of the shop, and the general scandal of poisoned chocolates. Ally could see people driving slowly past the cottage as she readied Arnold for his walk. She had already placed a call to the lawyer and made an appointment to see him. By taking Arnold for a walk she hoped that she would run into someone from Myrtle's family, or even her ex. Also, it might be her last chance to take Arnold for a walk for a long time.

"Ally, hold on, let me get my shoes and I'll come with you."

Ally snapped the leash onto Arnold's collar then waited in front of the cottage for her grandmother. As she did, a car slowed down in front of the house and then stopped.

"What are you doing here?"

Ally raised an eyebrow and tried to peer

through the window. The sunlight hit it just the right way to prevent her from seeing who the driver was.

"I live here."

"Shouldn't you be in jail?" The driver leaned over and out of the sunlight. Ally saw that it was Jensen, the security guard from the night before. She had forgotten to ask her grandmother if she knew who he was.

"That's none of your business."

"Isn't it? You broke into one of the apartments in my building."

"You did your job, now just move along." Ally tightened her grip on the pig's leash.

"You still have that guy?"

"Who are you?" Ally stared at him.

"Oh, you really don't remember, do you?" He chuckled. "I don't blame you. But, I bet after last night you won't be able to forget."

"Maybe you could just tell me?"

"What would be the fun in that, Ally?" He tilted his head to the side. "So, I guess you have an in with the detective. Are you seeing him or something?"

"Why would I answer that? I have no idea who you are."

"All right, then." He shrugged. "Don't let me catch you breaking in again. Got it?"

Ally stared at him. He had a strange way of speaking to her, as if he knew her quite well. "I don't think you have to worry about that." She didn't add the reason why. She would be in jail by the end of the day.

"Good. Because I take my job very seriously." He started to drive off.

"Wait!" Ally ran up to the car.

"What is it?"

"Did you notice anyone visiting Myrtle or arguing with her?"

"You mean other than Ruth?" He laughed. "No. Nice old ladies don't usually have too many enemies. Of course, nice young ladies don't usually break into apartments either." He winked at her and then drove away. Ally was unsettled, but she couldn't pinpoint why. It was odd to have someone know her, when she couldn't recall who they were. She vowed to ask her grandmother about him and look through her yearbook before she was carted off to jail.

"Who was that, Ally?" Charlotte stepped outside.

"The security guard from Freely Lakes."

"Oh? Is he a good guy?"

Ally squinted after the retreating car. "I'm not sure yet. He seems to remember me."

"Maybe someone you went to school with?"

"I think so. His name is Jensen," Ally said. "Do you know him?" Charlotte thought for a minute.

"Doesn't ring a bell."

"Anyway, he reminded me that there is one particular person that obviously had it in for

Myrtle. Ruth."

"Oh yes!" Charlotte gasped. "And she would have known how much Myrtle liked the chocolates."

"Let's take Arnold for a walk, then once we take him back home I think you should pay Ruth a visit."

"Me?" Charlotte asked.

"I think it's probably best if I don't set foot on Freely Lake's property."

"Okay. I knew there was more to the story about last night. Anything you want to tell me?" Charlotte asked.

"Nothing to worry about." Ally shrugged. She didn't want to burden her grandmother with her impending arrest.

As they walked towards the center of town Ally's thoughts returned to Jensen. She imagined that was a last name not a first name. But no matter how she scoured her memory she couldn't recall meeting a boy with the last name of Jensen while she was in school. It was a bit strange that he remembered her, if she didn't remember him. A taxi whizzed past them. In most towns a taxi might not be noticed, but in their little town, it was an unusual sight. Not many people needed a taxi to get to places and even fewer would take one to or from the airport as usually family or friends would have that honor.

"I bet that's one of Myrtle's children. Let's see if we can catch up with them." Ally started walking faster.

"We should be cautious though. If they know anything about how their mother died, they might hold it against us."

"Maybe." Ally tightened her grip on Arnold's leash. He was rooting around in a neighbor's garden.

When they reached town Ally looked around for the taxi. She spotted it parked outside one of the local breakfast cafés. It was easy to see through the big front window.

"That's him, that's Mark. And look, Myrtle's

daughter is with him," Charlotte said eagerly.

"If they're in there then they have already been updated by the town gossips about the shop being shut down," Ally said. "Let me go in to talk to them."

"Are you sure?"

"Yes, I don't want to put you in that position. When we were at the open house I heard that the nail salon is having a special for Freely Lake's residents today. Why don't you see if any of the residents are there? Maybe they can give you some information, maybe about the feud between Ruth and Myrtle. We can leave Arnold here for a few minutes."

"All right. But, be careful what you say to Myrtle's kids. We don't want to cast more suspicion on ourselves."

"I'll do my best." Ally smiled.

As her grandmother walked away Ally tied Arnold's leash to a lamp post. Ally stepped into the café. The moment that she did, the lively din died down to a subtle clink of silverware. Ally cleared her throat and walked towards the table where Myrtle's children were seated. "Excuse me, I'm sorry to bother you. I just wanted to say how sorry I am about your loss."

The two looked at her.

"Did you know my mother?" Mark gestured for her to sit down beside him. Ally took the invitation though it led to several glares from others in the café.

"Not well. I had just met her before she passed. My grandmother knew her better."

"Your grandmother?"

"Charlotte Sweet."

"Wait. The owner of the chocolate shop?" He asked as his eyes narrowed with anger. Ally could tell that this was not going to go as she had hoped.

"Yes," Ally answered cautiously.

"How dare you sit down with us?" Myrtle's son glared at her. "We know what you did to our mother!"

"Now wait, please. We had nothing to do with it. We're trying to figure out who did."

"I'm sure." Mark shook his head. "It took some nerve to walk in and speak to us."

"I only did it because I really want to help. I want to find out what happened to your mother. I was hoping you might know if your mother had any problems with anyone."

"Only the people who gave her poisoned candy!" Mark gestured to the waitress. "Bring the check please."

"Mark wait, I'm hungry, and you know that Aunt Stephanie can't cook," Shirley said.

"I've lost my appetite, I don't know how you can eat when this woman is here."

"Listen, Mom never had anything but good things to say about Charlotte. The police will find out the truth."

"Yes, they will," Ally agreed. She was sure that when she was taken away in handcuffs later that day all of the judgmental stares from around the restaurant would be vindicated. "I'm just trying to understand why anyone would want to hurt your mother. She seemed like such a nice person."

"She was a nice person. Not exactly an emotional person, but nice," Shirley said.

"So she didn't have anyone upset with her?" Ally asked.

"Not that I know about," Shirley said. "She wasn't exactly the sharing type though. I know she had some trouble with one of the other residents there. Ruth."

"Oh yes." Ally nodded. "I noticed that there was some tension there. Did your mother ever mention why?"

"As far as I could tell it was all over her apartment," Shirley said. "This Ruth wanted the one my mother had. I guess at some point she flat out refused, and from then on Ruth caused her problems. It upset my mother that she spread rumors that she was dying."

"I think that would upset anyone," Ally said.

Mark seemed to be relaxing in Ally's presence. "It upset her more because she once had a scare." He frowned. "Got diagnosed with a terminal illness and they thought she was going to die. It's why she and our father split up."

"Oh?" Ally met his eyes. "He didn't want to take care of her?"

"Exactly the opposite. She didn't want to be taken care of, by anyone. When she was diagnosed the doctor told her she had only months to live. So she wrote out a bucket list and divorced my father. He begged her to stay, to get treatment, to let him take care of her, but she said she could never do that. You know her own parents died when she was young, and she had to take care of her little sister. Maybe that had something to do with it. Anyway, it all turned out to be a misdiagnosis, but by then the divorce was final. I guess it was hard for her when Ruth started spreading those rumors. It probably reminded her of that time in her life."

"Plus, it's just rude." Shirley shook her head.

"I thought people got kinder with age, but I guess not."

"Aunt Stephanie certainly hasn't." Mark chuckled.

"Your mother's sister? Is she not kind to you?" Ally looked between the two.

"She's nice enough to us, but she and my mother didn't always get along," Mark said.

"Really?" Ally raised an eyebrow.

"Sure. See, my mother's parents left her a large sum of money that was meant to help her care for Aunt Stephanie. Which she did. But she never shared any of it with Aunt Stephanie."

"Oh wow, did they have a falling out about it? I saw her at the open house with your mother," Ally said.

"Oh, I'm sure she was there. Even though they didn't always get along they were still sisters and were close. I mean Aunt Stephanie knew she would get her money when Mom died," Shirley said. "Aunt Stephanie hated her old job and she hated managing the convenience store even more. Especially because Mom could retire early." All of a sudden Ally remembered that she knew Stephanie because she worked at the convenience store.

"How funny it will be when they read the will?" Mark said.

"What's so funny about the will?" Ally leaned closer.

"Oh nothing." Mark shrugged with a slight grin. "Now, if you don't mind, we're trying to enjoy our meal."

Ally was reminded that Mark was not interested in being very friendly to her.

"All right, I'll be on my way. Again, I am very sorry for your loss, and if there's anything..."

"Please, don't." Mark glared at her. "Don't offer to help us when it was chocolates from your grandmother's shop that killed our mother. I'm trying to be civil here."

Ally nodded and edged away from the table.

She stepped out of the café and right into a mess.

"Who in the world thinks it's okay to leave a pig outside a café?" Stephanie stomped a foot against the sidewalk. "That ugly, smelly thing belongs on a farm, not a sidewalk."

"I'm so sorry, I just stepped in for a minute." Ally cringed when she saw that Arnold had dug his snout into a flower pot. There was soil and flowers scattered everywhere.

"Get him out of here before I call the pound!"

"That won't be necessary, I'll clean up the mess." Ally smiled slightly.

"And who will repair my morning? Here I am trying to grieve the loss of my sister and I have to deal with running into this pig."

"I'm very sorry. I'm sorry for your loss as well."

"I bet you are. Aren't you the same person that brought the chocolates to the open house? The chocolates that my sister ate?" She raised her voice, which drew the attention of everyone around her. "The chocolates that were poisoned?"

"That's not true. The chocolates we brought to the open house were not poisoned," Ally insisted.

"Oh then, I guess the police got it wrong?"

"No, there were poisoned chocolates, but not from our shop."

"Oh, of course not. Because everyone here knows that Myrtle bought any old chocolates. Only that was not the case at all. In fact, the only place she bought chocolates from was your grandmother's shop."

"Stephanie, I'm sorry that your sister passed away, I really am, but it was not our chocolates that killed her."

"Well, I guess we'll just see about that when we find out who gets taken away in handcuffs, won't we, Ally?" She raised an eyebrow. Ally was a little surprised that Stephanie knew her name. She cleared her throat and tugged at Arnold's leash.

"I'm sure that the investigation will lead to the

truth."

"I'm sure it will." Stephanie brushed past her and into the café. As Ally did her best to clean up the mess Arnold had made she hoped that her grandmother was having better luck.

***

Charlotte pushed open the door to the nail salon. It was teeming with customers. One stood out because of her regal posture and odoriferous perfume. "Ruth?"

"Hmm?" The woman spun around with a toothy smile. When she saw Charlotte her smile faded. "What is it that you want?"

"I just wondered if I could speak to you for a moment."

"Sure." She stepped away from the crowd of women she was chatting with. "What is this about?"

"To be clear, Ruth, I'm hoping that you can give me some insight about Myrtle."

"Tragic." She shook her head.

“I couldn’t help but notice that you were pretty upset with Myrtle at the open house.”

“Wouldn’t you be upset if someone was saying bad things about you to the entire world?”

“Freely Lakes isn’t the entire world.”

“It might as well be. Everyone tiptoed around Myrtle like she was something so special. But she was a mean, old thing. I offered her twice what she paid for that apartment so that I could have a room with a view and she turned me down.”

“Maybe she liked the apartment,” Charlotte said.

“Maybe. But that’s no reason to be difficult. I even promised her that I would let her come over for lunch every day. I mean what more could she want?”

“The apartment that she purchased.”

“Look, I just wanted to be able to enjoy my time there. No one else would even talk about handing over their apartment. If she was so determined to keep it then she shouldn’t have gotten my hopes up."

"What do you mean?"

"I mean at first she told me yes, she would do it. She said it would give her the chance to put more money away for her kids. Then, all of a sudden that changed. She said she was changing her will and no longer needed to make more money."

"Why do you think that was?"

"I don't really know. Her son came to visit, then after that she blew me off. I tried to be nice about it, but I was really counting on getting that apartment. So, I was not too happy. I tried to convince her that selling to me was the right thing to do. She stopped taking my calls and answering her door. That's when I assumed she must be dying. I didn't want anyone else to try to lay claim to the apartment, so I left all kinds of hints with people that Myrtle was on death's door and the apartment was mine. I had no idea the rumors would get back to her."

"You didn't care too much if they did, did

you?" Charlotte said.

"Not much, no. Because I thought she was dying."

"And then you found out that she wasn't, so you decided to speed up the process?"

"Excuse me?" Ruth looked puzzled.

"You didn't want to wait anymore. You were counting on her dying, and when you found out that she wasn't and it was the reason she turned down your offer, you decided to take matters into your own hands. I mean, why wouldn't you? You had been patient enough."

"I wouldn't murder someone. You're just looking for someone to blame because those rancid chocolates killed someone. I have never touched the things myself. I don't know how people can pollute their bodies with all of that sugar. The way she ate them, she wouldn't have lived much longer, anyway. I saw she got some chocolates earlier in the day, and then I saw her sneaking away with one of the boxes from the food table at the open house. It's ridiculous. At her age, she should know better."

"Did you happen to notice who gave her the chocolates earlier in the day?"

"I don't know. I don't pay attention to the little people. Wouldn't you have an idea of who it might be? They were from your shop."

"Hmm, I can't recall, we sell lots of chocolates." Charlotte glanced at her watch. "Do you think you would like to get something to eat and we could talk about this more?"

"Eat? With you? I don't think so. You're being called the Chocolate Killer."

"You're joking."

"Not at all. Sorry hon, but my reputation can't handle being seen with you. Now, if you'll excuse me I need to shop for curtains for my new apartment."

As she walked away Charlotte clucked her tongue and muttered to herself, "Maybe she's not the murderer, but she's mean enough to be."

***

Ally had just scooped up the last of the soil from the flower pot when Charlotte walked up to her.

"What happened here?"

"Arnold."

"Oh, he does love to get into things doesn't he?" Charlotte replied hiding a smile.

"Did you find out anything?" Ally asked.

"Ruth was in there and I found out that she's mean enough to have murdered Myrtle, but I'm not convinced she did. How about Myrtle's kids?"

"Let's just say I wasn't very welcome at first. Although I found out a few tidbits about Myrtle's past. I think she might have changed her will. Maybe that's what the lawyer was for. It's just about time for the appointment with him. Do you think you could take Arnold home?"

"Sure. Ally, everyone in town seems to know about the chocolates being poisoned. We need to tread very carefully. I hope that Luke stands by his word and stays by your side."

"Some things are out of Luke's hands." Ally tried not to let her grandmother see what she was really thinking.

"Ally? Are you going to tell me the truth about last night?"

"There's nothing to worry about." Ally frowned. "Just make sure you feed Peaches, okay?"

"Okay." Charlotte looked as if she might say more, but Ally walked away fast. Ally knew if her grandmother pressed her she would give in and tell her the truth, but she wasn't ready to. She still held out hope that she would discover something before the arrest warrant was signed.

Chapter Eight

The lawyer's office was small and had a stale scent to it. Crammed into the tiny reception area was a desk and a bean pole of a woman. She looked up at Ally as Ally stepped inside.

"Ally Sweet?" Her nasally voice seemed to fill the small space.

"Yes."

"You are aware that Mr. Tweed is not a criminal lawyer?" Ally winced and nodded. So, Mr. Tweed already knew that she was a suspect. She doubted that he would be very forthcoming with information about his former client. "Okay, you can go in."

Ally moved past the desk and pushed the door open to the second part of the office. It was smaller than the reception area if that was possible. The man behind the desk had a bushy, white mustache, a mostly bald head, and was very short.

"Ms. Sweet, do come in and sit." He gestured to a wooden chair. Ally sat down in it. When she did her knees touched the front of his desk. "Now, what is it that I can do for you?"

"Well, I think you may know why I'm here."

"Unfortunately, I am not a criminal lawyer. I deal with estates, and finances."

"Like Myrtle's will?"

He tensed. "I'm not at liberty to discuss that."

"Surely, with her passing, she wouldn't mind."

"I don't know that."

"I do know that she would have a very big problem with the owner and manager of her favorite chocolate shop being framed for her murder."

"Hmm, you're just going to lay it all on the table?" He smiled slightly.

"Well, it's what you've heard right? I don't know how much time I have before I'm behind bars, and I'd like the truth. Were you changing

Myrtle's will?"

He frowned. "If word gets out that I divulge client information, people won't trust me."

"I'm not going to tell anyone. I just want to know, would anyone in her family have reason to be angry with her?"

"Sure. People don't like it when a rich person leaves them nothing. Hypothetically."

"Of course. So, maybe her kids?"

"I can't speak to that."

"I need your help, Mr. Tweed."

"No, Ms. Sweet you need the help of a criminal lawyer, a good one. I could recommend one if you would like."

"I guess it couldn't hurt."

"Ask June to get you a business card for Chris Tussons. He'll take good carc of you."

"You really won't tell me anything about the will?"

"I'm afraid not."

Ally stood up from the chair. She could see that Mr. Tweed was not going to budge. She left his office and found June chatting on the phone.

"I'm telling you it's Ally Sweet. Oops, I have to go." She hung up the phone. Ally pursed her lips.

"Mr. Tweed said you could give me a business card for Chris Tussons."

"Oh sure. He's great." She glanced around her messy desk. "But you know, I think I left his business cards in Mr. Tweed's office. If you'll excuse me for just a minute." She stood up and edged her way around the desk. As she did, she knocked into a large pile of paperwork. She caught it just before it fell.

"Ugh, I've got to get around to filing these. I never have the time." Ally refrained from pointing out that filing might be a priority over gossiping on the phone.

The moment the woman stepped into Mr. Tweed's office Ally started to sort through the paperwork. If June was behind on filing there was a good chance that Myrtle's paperwork was in the pile. She didn't have to dig far before she came across it. With the will being read the next day, Ally couldn't steal the paper. She pulled out her phone and snapped a picture of every page she could get to before the door swung open. Ally was in such a rush to back away that she knocked the pile of papers to the floor.

"Oh no!" June sighed. "I guess I have my work cut out for me. Anyway, here's the card." She held the card out to Ally. Ally took the card.

"I'm sorry about the mess. Would you like some help?" Ally offered.

"No please, it will be easier to do when there is only one person in here."

Ally nodded and walked out of the office. She paused in front of the building and looked down at the card in her hand. Maybe she really should give him a call. After all, at any moment a patrol car could come screaming up to her with Luke in the front seat. She wondered whether he would be there, or if he would leave it to a couple of officers so that he did not have to witness it. As much as she wanted to avoid it, she did need to prepare for the worst.

When she pulled out her phone to dial the number on the business card she saw the picture she had taken of the paperwork. It was a will. It was a very short and simple will. It stated that Myrtle's apartment and its contents were to be sold. The proceeds from that sale and all of her remaining funds and assets were to be donated to charity. Not a dime had been left to a single family member. The list of likely suspects in Myrtle's murder had just expanded. Her sister Stephanie, her ex-husband Nate, and her two dear children, might all have motive. The question was, had the will been finalized before Myrtle's death?

***

When Ally got back to the cottage her mind was still reeling from her encounter with the lawyer. She opened the door to find her grandmother inside. She had just set food down for Arnold and Peaches.

"Ally, there you are. How did the meeting go?"

"Not great." Ally shook her head. "I'm not sure that we're going to get anything solid on the will. I was lucky to find a copy of it, she changed it to leave all of her wealth to charity, but I have no way of knowing if it was completed before she passed away."

"Wow. Well, that's enough to give that whole family motive, hmm?"

"I think you're right about that."

"Do you think there's anything that Luke can do to help you find out about whether the will was finalized?"

"There might be, but he is not in the most cooperative mood."

"Why is that?" Charlotte asked.

"He's still quite upset about the break-in. In fact, I think he's downright angry."

"Well, it was a risky move, not just for us, but for the case itself."

"But we did find our chocolates hidden, remember?" Ally said.

"I wonder why Myrtle did that."

"Maybe she didn't want to share?"

"Or maybe, someone else wanted her to eat the other chocolates," Charlotte suggested.

"They were wrapped with the ribbon we use for delivery," Ally explained. "Did you have a chance to look through all of the recent orders for delivery?"

"The police seized all of the paperwork," Charlotte said.

"What about the computer?"

"Oh Ally, you know I don't keep that thing up to date."

"Hm. We could check with Brian, he's the one that makes the deliveries," Ally suggested.

"We could, but he quit when the shop got shut down. Said he couldn't risk losing his income so he had to find another job," Charlotte said.

"Oh wow, I didn't realize."

"So, we're at a dead end unless we call him."

"Maybe not. Don't all of the deliveries get programmed into the GPS?" Ally asked.

"Yes, but we don't even know what day they were delivered. The GPS only holds the recent deliveries." Charlotte looked thoughtful.

"It's a place to start." Ally sighed.

"All right, why don't you head into the shop and check the GPS? I'm going to make a few calls to see if I can get the shop reopened."

"Calls? To whom?" Ally asked.

"I have my connections." Charlotte winked at her.

Ally walked to the shop. As she approached it she heard a few voices. She paused at the side of the building.

"Murder by chocolate?"

"Worse, murder by chocolate candy." Ally recognized Mrs. Cale's voice.

"I really don't think they had anything to do with it." That was Mrs. White.

"You never know. Some of your best friends can turn out to be serial killers."

"Wait a minute. Are you a serial killer?" Mrs. White said.

"No."

"Does that mean I'm a serial killer?"

"I don't know, are you?"

"I don't think so," Mrs. White replied.

"Well, then I guess not." Mrs. Cale laughed. Ally tried not to laugh at her words.

"All I'm saying is that it was their chocolates. The shop is closed. There's obviously evidence against them." Mrs. Cale clucked her tongue.

"I can't argue with that. The shop being closed sure does make them look guilty."

"I'm not sure if I'll ever be able to eat a chocolate from Charlotte's Chocolate Heaven again," Mrs. Cale concluded in a disparaging voice.

As the two women walked past, Ally sighed. If

even their most loyal customers had lost faith in them, what was the chance of the shop surviving?

She trudged around the back of the shop to the van. When she opened the door she was greeted by the smell of the disinfectant that the driver cleaned the van with every day. She leaned inside and grabbed the GPS. Just as Charlotte had predicted there were only a few addresses stored in the GPS. They were all addresses in Blue River or Mainbry. As she skimmed over them she noticed that one of the addresses was Freely Lakes. That wasn't unusual as they delivered there often. The GPS did not give a date of the delivery. It was yet another dead end.

After thinking about it for some time Ally decided to pay a visit to Freely Lakes. Since her car was at the cottage she decided to take the van. As she drove to the retirement community she noticed quite a few looks from people that she passed. She gritted her teeth and tried not to take it personally.

Chapter Nine

Ally waited in the small security office at Freely Lakes. A bank of computer monitors revealed how she had been caught so easily when she broke into Myrtle's room. The perimeter of the building appeared to be completely covered. The security officer had probably watched her climb the fire escape. Ally felt a sense of reassurance that it might not be such a dangerous place to live after all.

"Ally? What are you doing here?"

She turned to find the security guard filling the doorway. A quick skip of her heartbeat took her breath away. Even though she had been waiting for him she was still startled by his presence.

"I need to ask you a question."

"Is it about why I didn't press charges because I would have liked to if I could have."

"No." Ally frowned. "I need to know if you can

show me footage of recent deliveries."

He leaned against the frame of the door and looked at her with a quirked brow. "Are you kidding? What makes you think I would give you access to that?"

"I'm not here to argue. I just want to know when a delivery was made from our shop and who it was delivered to."

"Isn't that information that you should have?"

"It's a long story." She shook her head. "Just help me out here, please."

"You still don't remember me, do you?"

Ally stared at him. She wished that she could remember him, but nothing about him reminded her of anything other than being caught breaking and entering. "I'm sorry, no I don't. If I did something to upset you..."

"No. It wasn't like that. I just wasn't very noticeable. I'm Donovan. We were in the same class."

"Donovan?" She narrowed her eyes. "I don't

remember any Donovan…" She gasped. "Wait a minute, you mean Donny?"

"Okay yes, that was my nickname in school."

"Oh wow." Ally's eyes widened. "You look very different."

"It's amazing what contacts and weightlifting will do."

"Yes, it is." Ally grinned. "I mean, not that you didn't look fine then, it's just that I can't believe how you've changed."

"Please, you never gave me a second glance at school."

"Well, I didn't intentionally overlook you."

"No? Not with my thick glasses and my skinny arms?"

"Did I ever do anything to put you down?" Ally asked. "I only remember you as being very shy."

"Yes, I was shy, and no, you were one of the few people that didn't put me down. I guess it just stings a little not to be remembered by your high school crush."

"Crush?" Ally laughed. "Really?"

"Well, you don't have to be cruel about it."

"I'm sorry, I wasn't laughing because of that. I was laughing because it surprised me. I don't think you ever said more than three words to me."

"How could I? You were a cheerleader..."

"One year."

"And you were popular," Donovan continued.

"I wasn't that popular. I had a few friends, that was all."

"To me you were. I didn't have any friends."

"I'm sure that you had at least a couple," Ally said.

"No, I was very shy." He frowned. "Anyway, none of that matters now. I still don't know why you would think you're entitled to see any of the recordings."

"Look, I don't have to see them for myself. If you just watch the videos for me and tell me the information, then what will that be violating?"

He narrowed his eyes. Ally was sure that he wasn't going to be swayed. After all, he had caught her committing a crime.

"All right. But only because I'm sure that you and your grandmother had nothing to do with this."

"Thanks Donny."

"It's Donovan now," he emphasized.

"Oops sorry. Thanks Donovan." He nodded and turned to the bank of monitors. "Start from the day of the open house and work your way back. I mean, if you don't mind."

"Sure." He glanced over his shoulder. As the first video began to play Ally's eyes widened.

"Look! It's right there."

He turned back to look at the screen just as the delivery van from the shop pulled up. The driver parked the van and carried the small box of chocolates into the building.

"Can you tell what room he went to?"

"Unfortunately, not from the video. He would have signed the log book, though." He walked over to a filing cabinet and opened one of the drawers. He pulled out a folder and began sorting through the papers inside. "That's weird." He looked puzzled.

"What is?"

"There's no information entered for any delivery from your shop on that day." He looked up at her.

"So, on the day of the open house there were chocolates delivered, but there's no entry?"

"It seems so, maybe someone made a mistake?" Donovan said. "I'll ask around and see if I can find out more information."

"Okay, thank you, Donovan."

"No problem, Ally. If there's any other way I can help just let me know. All right?"

"Sure. Thank you." She nodded as she walked out of the security office. She was surprised that his attitude towards her seemed to change so quickly. Her thoughts were heavy with frustration. When she reached the delivery van, she paused to make a phone call.

"Luke Elm."

"Luke, it's Ally."

"Oh?"

She grimaced at his tone. "I need you to check the records from the shop for me, please."

"Those are being searched at the moment," Luke replied in a businesslike tone.

"Great, then it should be no trouble to look up a delivery that took place on the day of the open house, to Freely Lakes."

"Ally." Luke's voice tightened. "You do realize that if I find that delivery it will only further implicate you."

"I'm trying to figure out who sent the chocolates, Luke. At this point it's pretty clear that every ounce of information is pointing towards our shop. So, I'd like to know who made the order, because they may just be the real killer."

"You think that someone ordered the chocolates, had them delivered, and then swapped them for the poisoned ones?"

"I think it's possible. It would have to be someone who had access to the chocolates. Someone at Freely Lakes."

"What about your delivery driver?"

"Seriously?"

"Well, he would have had access to the chocolates before they were delivered."

Ally sighed. "No, I don't think he would do that."

"We never think of the people around us as being capable of murder, Ally. But many times it is the people that we think we know the best that surprise us the most."

"I agree, but I don't think that's the case this time. I just need the information, Luke. Can't you get it for me?"

"I'll see what I can do, Ally, but you have to understand that I have to be careful about this case. I can't risk anyone thinking I tainted the evidence in any way. Especially with our..." he paused.

"Our?"

"Well you know, our friendship."

"You're saying you don't want anyone to think that your connection with me hindered your ability to arrest me for murder?"

"Ally. I told you before, I'm not going to arrest you."

"No, you're just going to get someone else to do it."

Luke took a sharp breath and cleared his throat. "You've got to give me a break here, Ally. You're handing them a case against you by taking chances that you shouldn't take, and somehow you expect me to be able to just ignore that? I do have a job to do. I was able to delay the arrest warrant, but it took quite a song and dance on my part, and I absolutely have to find a more viable suspect. You know, one that isn't actively providing more evidence of guilt."

Ally's heartbeat quickened. She wasn't sure if she was angry at Luke or angry at herself, but she was definitely angry.

"And I have a job to do, too, but I can't do it, because you shut down the shop."

"I didn't shut it down, I was given the order to. Besides, how would you feel if someone else got poisoned and we hadn't closed it? I wouldn't have shut it unless I absolutely had to. You know that. Don't you?" Luke asked.

"I do. I think. I'm just really stressed about all of this. See what you can do about finding out who the delivery was ordered by and who it was delivered to, please."

"I will. Ally, just try to let me sort this out. I'm sure I can get to the bottom of it, but the more evidence you create against yourself, the harder my job becomes. I understand why you are so concerned, but I need you to let me handle this."

"You do what you need to do, Luke. I

appreciate that you're looking out for me. But I have to do what I have to do, too."

"Ally, don't say I didn't warn you."

Ally frowned as she hung up the phone. One thing was for sure, she didn't want Luke to be the one who put the handcuffs on her. As angry as she was, she did appreciate that he seemed to care. However, all of that caring was not going to erase the pile of evidence that was mounting against her.

Chapter Ten

Ally started the van and drove back towards the shop, with the same judgmental stares following after her. As she parked outside the shop she remembered the smudges on her newly cleaned window. Had the killer been looking inside? Was it possible that the killer was watching her for quite some time? She shivered at the thought.

Ally looked at the shop and sighed. It was hard to think of a place so filled with love being linked to such a terrible crime. She looked at the closed sign on the shop door. It made her stomach ache to think that the doors might never reopen.

Ally was still in a funk when she got back to the cottage. Charlotte was nowhere to be seen when she stepped inside. Ally was a little relieved as she didn't want to explain her bad attitude. When she noticed a light on inside her grandmother's room she walked towards her door and knocked lightly.

"Come in!" Charlotte called out. Ally pushed the door open to find her grandmother surrounded by boxes.

"What are you doing?"

"I'm packing." Charlotte turned and smiled at her. "I think I've made a lot of progress."

"Mee-Maw, you're not really thinking of going through with the move, are you?"

"Well, of course. I don't see a reason not to."

"How about the fact that we are still being focused on as suspects in this murder?" Ally asked.

"Oh, Ally don't worry about that. You know that you didn't do it, you know that I didn't do it, so what is there to worry about?"

"According to Luke, quite a bit."

"Those law enforcement types are always a little highly strung. You just have to let it roll off your back." Charlotte smiled comfortingly.

"Mee-Maw, I don't think you're taking this seriously enough."

"If I thought there was an issue, don't you think I would be doing everything to fix it?" Charlotte dropped a pair of shoes into one of the boxes. "I don't want to lose my opportunity to move into Freely Lakes and if I don't start planning ahead I'm going to have a slew of packing to do. Besides, I find the best way to prevent getting down in the dumps about a problem is for me to keep busy. Normally, I would make chocolates, but well, you know."

"Yes, I do." Ally shook her head. "I wish I could be as calm as you, Mee-Maw."

"I may look calm now, but if I find out that Luke's coming after you, you're going to see a whole other person."

Ally laughed at the thought. She had seen that whole other person quite a few times in her lifetime, and she had to admit that Charlotte on a rampage was frightening, even to her.

"I'm going to go lay down for a bit."

"Looking up the delivery information didn't go well?"

“No, not well at all. I know that chocolates from our shop were delivered to Freely Lakes on the day of the open house, but not to whom, or who they were ordered by.”

“Wait a minute. On the day of the open house?”

“Yes. I saw the CCTV footage from Freely Lakes myself.”

“But we didn’t even open the shop that day.”

Ally blinked. “So, why would Brian be making a delivery?”

“I think that’s a very good question.”

“I’ll give Brian a call and check it out.”

“Ally, try not to worry too much. It’s all going to be just fine. I think there’s a lot more to worry about in life than the things that will work themselves out.”

“I wish I had your positive outlook, Mee-Maw.”

“It’s something that comes with age.” Charlotte laughed.

Ally left her grandmother's room and returned to her own. When she stepped inside, Peaches pranced right over to her. She rubbed her cheek against Ally's hand when she reached down to pet her.

"You can always tell when I need you, can't you, Peaches?" She picked her up and cradled her in her arms. After petting the cat for a few minutes she called the delivery driver. He answered on the fourth ring.

"Ally? I already told Charlotte..."

"I know, I know. It's okay. But I have a question for you."

"Sure, what is it?"

"Did you make a delivery to Freely Lakes on the day of the open house?"

"No, I don't think so," he said.

"But the van was at Freely Lakes on that day. I saw the video footage and you got out of the van and took in some chocolates."

"Oh, now I remember."

"And?" Ally asked. She was starting to get a bit impatient.

"I was visiting my grandmother," he said.

"The chocolates were for your grandmother?" Ally asked.

"I paid for the chocolates," he said defensively.

"Oh, that's okay I'm sure you did, that's not the problem."

"Grandma Ruth said she needed them for a gift."

"Grandma Ruth," Ally's head spun at the realization. Ruth got chocolates delivered from the shop on the day that Myrtle was murdered. Could she have swapped them to kill Myrtle?

"Ally, are you there?" he asked.

"Yes, sorry," Ally muttered. "Do you know who they were a gift for?"

"No, sorry Ally," he said. "I was just using the van like Charlotte let me when she doesn't need it. I was going to visit my grandmother anyway. I hope that's okay."

"That's okay, thanks." Ally wanted to ask more questions, but she didn't want to outright accuse his grandmother of murder.

Ally hung up and bit into her bottom lip. Peaches purred and nuzzled her elbow. She stroked the cat's fur. "Well, Peaches I wonder if those chocolates were given to Myrtle. They certainly hated each other. Now I just need to see if I can find out?"

Peaches meowed and bumped the top of her head against Ally's palm. "I know, I know, I'm not supposed to worry, but how can I not worry?" She shook her head and closed her eyes. "I can't imagine how someone could despise us enough to try to frame us for murder." She pulled Peaches closer. "You always help me calm down, but I'm not sure if it's going to work this time." Peaches curled up in her lap and nestled her chin in her paws. Ally pet her. Slowly she did begin to relax. "Honestly Peaches, I can't imagine that after all of this Luke is going to want anything to do with me.

I guess that's for the best. My relationships haven't been very successful."

Peaches flicked her with her tail. "Okay, our relationship has been very successful." She smiled and scratched the cat's chin. She just hoped they would be able to clear their names so Peaches wouldn't have to visit her in jail.

Chapter Eleven

Ally was still thinking about the conversation she had with the delivery driver when there was a knock on her bedroom door.

"Ally?"

"Come in, Mee-Maw." She felt a pang of disappointment that soon they would not be able to just knock on each other's door. Charlotte opened the door and peeked in at her.

"I was afraid you might be sleeping."

"No. I think I just found our murderer."

"Really?"

"I just found out that Brian delivered the chocolates to Freely Lakes on the day of the murder to his grandmother, Ruth, so she could give them as a gift."

"What?" Charlotte's eyes widened. "Oh, of course. No, Brian's grandmother is not the Ruth we suspect. It is a different Ruth."

"Oh, Mee-Maw. What a coincidence. I didn't want to suspect that Brian or his family could somehow be involved. That's a relief, but it's another dead end. This is all such a mess, I'm not sure how we're going to pull out of it."

"Take a breath, Ally. It's going to be okay."

"But what if it's not?"

Charlotte sat down on the bed beside her. She took Ally's hand in her own. "We will always be okay, sweetheart. You have to stop looking at everything that is wrong, and start looking at everything that is right."

"What's right?"

"Luke's on our side."

"So far."

"I'm sure he will continue to be. Now come on, we can go for a walk, and you can fill me in on the delivery."

"A walk?" Ally shook her head. "The last thing I want is to see people in town. They will all be staring at us."

"So, let them stare. We have never been a family that shies away from that. Right?" Charlotte looked into her eyes. "Now is the time we have to be brave. If we hide away, then we'll be proving their suspicions right, that we have something to feel guilty about. Don't you think?"

"I guess."

"Let's just take a walk. Hmm? Fresh air can make everything better." Charlotte linked her arm through Ally's. Ally sighed. She still didn't think it was a good idea. But her grandmother was right. If she stayed inside all she would do was wallow. That was something that Charlotte never allowed. No matter what difficulty she faced, Ally was always pulled to her feet and forced to deal with it head on. Even as an adult, things were no different.

"Let's go, let's go." Charlotte patted her arm. "Arnold needs a walk you know."

"I know, I know." When they walked into the kitchen Arnold snorted impatiently. "Don't worry we didn't forget about you, Piggie." Ally patted his head and then clipped the leash onto Arnold's collar. As they stepped outside it was just dusk.

"Maybe a walk really isn't a good idea," Ally said, still trying to get out of it.

"Nonsense. We have to keep our health, and that means exercise."

Ally nodded and started walking. The further along the sidewalk that they traveled the happier Arnold became. When they neared the shops Arnold really snorted.

"He must like all the smells in the air." Charlotte smiled fondly at him. Arnold pulled hard on his leash. Ally tried to pull back, but the pig was determined. One thing Ally learned real fast about Arnold was that when he wanted something, it was best just to let him have it. In the long run the fight was not worth the stress. She let him lead her along to the back of the convenience store. She sighed impatiently when he shoved his snout into a trashcan that had been tipped over, perhaps by other larger animals. He snorted and grunted as he dug deeper into the trash.

"Arnold, cut it out." Ally frowned. She still wasn't in the best mood and Arnold certainly wasn't making it any better for her. She tried to tug him back, but he refused and snorted louder. Ally dropped down to one knee and tried to guide Arnold away from the trash. As she pushed his kicking and squealing body away from the trash she noticed that something strange clung to his snout. It was an empty package of walnuts. Ally stared at the wrapper.

"Look at this, Mee-Maw." She held it out for her grandmother to see.

"Interesting. They could have been used in the chocolates."

"This is it! Stephanie must be the killer."

"Slow down, sh." Charlotte looked around to see if anyone was close enough to hear Ally. "We don't know that for sure. This is a convenience store maybe she just sells them."

"Well, if she does maybe we can find out if she

remembers who bought them recently."

"It couldn't hurt to ask." Charlotte tucked the wrapper into her purse. Ally led Arnold around the corner to the front of the store. Stephanie opened the door with her keys in hand.

"Sorry ladies, just closing up."

"Oh, I just need one thing for a recipe, Stephanie, could I just duck in and get it?" Charlotte said sweetly.

"What is it?" Stephanie raised an eyebrow.

Charlotte reached into her purse and pulled out the packaging. "This kind of walnuts."

To Ally it seemed that Stephanie's face paled when she saw the wrapper, but maybe she was just imagining it. "Where did you get that?"

"Do you carry them? Please, I just need one bag," Charlotte said.

"I'm sorry we're closed. You can come back tomorrow. Or better yet hit the grocery store. It's still open for an hour and they carry a variety of brands."

“We don’t have our car at the moment and I don’t want to walk that far. Maybe I could pick it up in the morning?” Charlotte asked.

Stephanie locked the door. “You’re better off going to the grocery store. I carry a lot of products, even if that’s one of them, I can’t guarantee that I have it in stock.”

Arnold snorted and tried to sniff Stephanie’s shoes. The closer he got to them the more excited he became. Ally tried to tug him back.

“Could you please make him stop?” Stephanie moved her foot as if she might kick Arnold. Ally moved fast to lean down and shield him. Her hand brushed across Stephanie’s shoe as she reached for the pig. Ally pulled him away.

“Sorry,” she said, but she shot a glare of warning at Stephanie. The very idea that someone might try to hurt Arnold made her very angry.

“Just keep control of him. Who has a pig for a pet, anyway?” She shook her head and turned to walk away. Ally tried to peer through the front window to see if the brand of walnuts was on the shelf. When she brushed her hand across the window she noticed that she left a dark smudge behind. After all the trouble she had with keeping the front window clean she was sensitive to smudged windows.

"Ugh, she must have had dirt on her shoe." Ally turned her hand to the side and saw a large smear of brown across the side of her hand.

"Oh gross, is that mud or something worse?"

Charlotte leaned close and sniffed. "Relax, it's chocolate."

"No wonder Arnold was going nuts. He must have smelled the chocolate."

"Here." Charlotte handed her a tissue to clean her hand with. "What would Stephanie be doing with chocolate on her shoes?"

"I don't know, but between the walnuts and the chocolate, I'm starting to think that she had something to do with her sister's death."

"Maybe, but it doesn't prove anything. Let's follow her a bit and see where she ends up. It'll be fun." Charlotte winked at Ally. Ally grinned.

"Mee-Maw, we have to talk about your version of fun."

"Sh. Look, she's going away from the parking lot." Charlotte pointed out Stephanie's bright red jacket. She was walking towards the small patch of woods.

"What is she going back there for?" Ally frowned.

"We're going to find out."

Ally and Charlotte walked across the parking lot to the other side. Then they followed Stephanie into the trees. Stephanie was still several feet ahead of them when they heard a male voice.

"We shouldn't be meeting like this. Not with the kids in town."

"I had to see you. What are we going to do?" Stephanie asked.

"The same thing I told you to do. We just need time for things to die down."

"I don't know, Nate, I just want to move on

with our lives." Ally and Charlotte looked at each other when they heard his name. Was this Myrtle's ex-husband?

"Relax, the process takes time. We don't want to make a mistake and be caught."

"I know, but I just want to have Myrtle's murder behind us?"

"It will be soon enough."

"What happens if the kids figure us out?" Stephanie asked.

"It's okay we'll just tell them the truth."

Ally held her breath. She wanted to hear a full confession. Instead she heard the unmistakable sound of lips smacking in a kiss. Her mouth fell open in shock. Stephanie and her sister's ex-husband? It made her feel uncomfortable to even consider it.

"Nate, I wish we didn't have to wait so long."

"Me too, Stephanie, but they just lost their mother."

"Some mother."

"She was a hard woman, but she was their mother. They don't need anything else to shake up their lives right now. They will find out eventually, and as much as they love you, I'm sure they will find a way to accept it."

"I hope so." Stephanie sniffled.

"Don't cry my love. It's all right. Everything is falling into place now, hmm?"

"You're right. I'm sorry. It's just that I feel like I'm being followed, or watched, or something."

Ally and Charlotte exchanged a glance. Suddenly a little mouse raced by Arnold. Arnold let out a loud snort and tried to chase after it. Ally did her best to hold onto his leash, but she wasn't expecting him to bolt and didn't have a good grip. He rushed off through the woods after the mouse.

"Arnold!" Ally tried to cry out, but Charlotte put a hand over her mouth to quiet her.

"Who's there?" Nate shouted. Then there was a rustling of leaves as the two ran off through the woods. Charlotte let go of Ally and Ally rushed through the woods to find Arnold. She searched everywhere, but there was no sign of him. Her eyes filled with tears as she realized that she had lost her grandmother's beloved pet.

"Ally, come out of there. We need to go home."

"But, Mee-Maw, I didn't find Arnold!"

"Arnold will come home on his own. He's gotten away from me before. Even pigs need a little freedom now and then." Charlotte smiled at her granddaughter. "Just come home with me, then we'll go looking for him in the morning."

"What if that awful woman, Stephanie, gets hold of him?"

"I think Stephanie has bigger problems right now."

"I know. What did you think about their conversation? I thought they might be talking about the murder."

"Maybe. But they didn't say anything really incriminating, other than the fact that they are lovers and trying to hide it. That doesn't make them criminals or murderers."

"No, but it does give them motive. Especially, if they knew that Myrtle was about to change her will."

"The question is, did they know? She might have confided in her sister, but we don't know that for sure."

"You're right," Ally agreed. "Maybe I just got caught up in the fact that she was trying to kick Arnold."

"There is still the wrapper." Charlotte patted her purse. "Maybe that will lead us somewhere."

"I'll check in with Luke in the morning."

"Good idea."

"If he'll take my call."

"I'm sure he will be fine, Ally. I know I was upset with him at first, but really Luke was just doing his job. I'm sure he's working hard to get the shop reopened."

"I know you're right, but it's hard not to be

upset with him."

"Well, he didn't give us a hard time. He's tried to be helpful and I think he's just doing his job."

"I guess." Ally glanced over her shoulder several times as they walked back to the cottage. She kept hoping that Arnold would come running up to her.

"Try not to worry, Ally. Things always have a way of working out."

Ally nodded, but she still felt miserable. When she arrived home she closed herself off in her room and curled up with Peaches. She could feel the soothing vibrations of her purring. Ally began to relax.

"Peaches, you have to help me find Arnold. Okay?"

Peaches rubbed her cheek against Ally's and offered a soft meow. Ally smiled. She pet the cat and closed her eyes. All of her thoughts about the case swarmed through her mind. If she couldn't figure out who killed Myrtle, then she might not ever be able to repair the reputation of the chocolate shop in the community. It would take time and a very clear verdict for people to forget the scandal.

Chapter Twelve

The next morning Ally pulled herself out of bed without much enthusiasm. In fact she would have preferred to close her eyes and go right back to sleep. But she wanted to find out if Arnold had made it home. As she trudged out into the kitchen she could smell the coffee that her grandmother had already made.

"Did Arnold make it back yet?"

"No. I'm afraid not. But I'm sure that he'll come home when he gets hungry. Silly pig, he must think he's a cat, chasing after that mouse."

"It was pretty silly." Ally frowned. "I can't believe he took off like that. He's pretty fast for his size."

"He is a spirited swine."

"I know." Ally gazed out the window that overlooked the driveway. It took her a moment to recognize the car that pulled to a stop in front of the house. "Oh no, Luke's here and I'm still in my pajamas!"

"Relax, it's not the first time that he's seen you in your pajamas." Charlotte ran her fingers through Ally's hair and buttoned the top button of her pajama top. "There you go. You look ravishing."

"I'm sure," Ally said laughing. She felt very uncomfortable having to face Luke in her pajamas. However, there was no time to change as Luke was already out of the car. The sun shone on his hair, as usual, making him look like something crafted by the universe just for her. Instead of walking up the driveway to the front door of the cottage, Luke walked over to the back passenger door of his car. Ally raised an eyebrow as he opened the door. She watched him stumble and struggle with something. When he turned around he had Arnold's leash in his hand and the pig started dragging him towards the house.

"Arnold!" Ally no longer cared about how she looked. She rushed out the door and met Luke halfway up the driveway. "Oh, you found him, thank you so much!" As soon as Ally took Arnold's leash and bent down to his level, Arnold calmed down. He nuzzled her cheek and sniffed her hand. "Where did you find him?"

"Digging up Mrs. Penn's roses. I would have taken him in for criminal mischief, but the cuffs kept slipping off."

"Ha ha." Ally grinned. "Thank you, Luke."

"Of course." He tilted his head towards the door. "May I come in for a moment?"

"Yes, sure." Ally took Arnold to the door holding onto his leash. The door was still slightly open. Arnold pushed the door the rest of the way open with his snout. Ally stepped inside and Luke stepped in behind her.

"Oh, there's my boy!" Charlotte clapped her hands as she bent down to hug Arnold. "I bet you're starving. Let me get you some chow."

"I am a little hungry." Luke nodded. Charlotte and Ally looked at each other and laughed. "Oh, you meant the pig? Of course, sorry."

"I'll make you some chow, too, Luke, please have a seat." She gestured to the table. Luke settled into one of the chairs. Ally sat down across from him.

"Arnold isn't the only reason that I'm here. I also wanted to check on the two of you. I know all of this has been stressful, and that you probably see me as working against you. But I'm not." He looked between the two of them. "I want to do everything I can to make sure that this case gets solved quickly."

"That's very kind of you, Luke." Charlotte patted his shoulder.

Ally smiled at her grandmother and then looked back at Luke. "As for the case, we found some interesting information last night," Ally said.

"Oh?"

"Yes. As we told you the chocolates that were poisoned did not come from our shop. The walnut on top wasn't caramelized and was left whole. We found, actually Arnold found, a package for walnuts in the garbage of Stephanie's store, the convenience store."

"Interesting," Luke said. "But that doesn't prove anything."

"That's not all. She also had chocolate on her shoe."

"Are you sure it was chocolate?" Luke winced.

"Yes, I sniffed it!" Charlotte called out as she buttered a few muffins.

"You sniffed her shoe?" Luke looked over at her with a raised eyebrow.

"It's a long story. The point is, she has no reason to have chocolate on her shoe," Ally said.

"Unless she stepped on a pre-packaged brownie, or anything else chocolaty for that matter, and got chocolate on her shoe. As for the walnut packaging, that's not much to go on."

"I know, but I'm sure it's related to the murder," Ally said.

"Maybe it is, but it's a stretch," he said. "Thank you for the muffin."

"You're welcome. Coffee, dear?" Charlotte asked.

Luke looked at her with a half-curled lip. "Sure, thank you." As Charlotte went back to the coffee maker, Luke leaned towards Ally. "I thought she hated me."

"She's more forgiving than I am." Ally shrugged.

"Aw, I did find Arnold, I thought that might get me back in your good graces."

"Hmm, maybe it would, if you reopened the shop."

"Give me a better suspect, and I will." He looked into her eyes. "I mean it, Ally. I want that shop reopened as much as you do. It will mean that I have a real suspect."

"One other than me you mean?"

"Yes. Unfortunately, we don't have too many leads. There are plenty of suspicious people in her life, but no evidence to back-up those suspicions."

"Maybe this will help." Ally did her best to

smooth down her hair. “We overheard Stephanie and Nate, Myrtle’s ex-husband, the father of her children, fighting about something.”

“How?”

“Well uh, we might have followed them.”

He rubbed his hands together. “Okay.” His eyes narrowed. “I thought he was still out of town. Maybe he came back early for the funeral. What were they fighting about?”

“It seems that they are lovers,” Ally said.

“Why is that important? If Myrtle and Nate were already divorced why would it matter?”

“Oh, you must not be around very many women.” Charlotte set down his coffee. “A sister dating the ex? Not acceptable.”

“Okay, so it’s more acceptable to kill her?” Luke said.

“Maybe they heard about Myrtle trying to change her will. They thought they would stop her before she had the chance to change it.”

“Don’t think I haven’t considered that

possibility. However, what we need is hard evidence, not hearsay and assumptions. So far I don't have any of that," Luke said.

"Not even the fact that they were lovers?" Ally asked.

"Falling in love isn't illegal, Ally." Luke locked eyes with her. "As far as I know. It's also not news. I've had a few people tell me about their relationship."

"Oh." Ally sighed. "Then I guess we're left with a whole lot of nothing."

"Don't worry. There is no perfect murder." Luke smiled. "Whoever did this is going to make a mistake."

"Unfortunately, it has to be a mistake that is also evidence." Ally frowned. Luke gave the back of her hand a light tap.

"Don't give up on me now, Ally."

Ally smiled as she met his eyes. She hadn't really thought about the fact that he needed her to believe in him.

"Thanks Luke, it makes me feel a lot better knowing that you're on the case."

He smiled at her and stood up from the table. "Just give me a little time, Ally."

"I'm sure you will figure it all out." Ally stood up and walked him to the door. Luke lingered by the door.

"And I'm sure that you're not going to give up. So, just be careful, Ally. Please?" He held her gaze.

"Well, since you asked so nicely." She leaned in and pecked him on the cheek. The movement was impulsive and unexpected for both of them. Luke grinned as a hint of red rose in his cheeks. Ally laughed and glanced away from him. "Sorry, I guess I was just caught up in the moment."

"Don't be sorry. Please." He winked at her and then turned to walk down the driveway. Ally watched him for a moment, then closed the door. After she closed the door, Ally turned to face her grandmother.

"That's so sweet the way you talked to him,

Ally. I'm sure that he really appreciates your confidence in him."

"Well, I hope he does, but that's not the only way this case is getting solved."

"What do you mean?" Charlotte set down her cup of coffee before she even had a chance to take a sip.

"I mean, if it's hard evidence that Luke needs, then it's hard evidence we have to find."

"What are you suggesting?" Charlotte raised an eyebrow.

"I am suggesting that we do a few searches of our own. If Stephanie is involved and she had chocolate on her shoe, then she had to make those chocolates somewhere, and she might have even left behind a footprint of chocolate."

"Oh, Ally, that's a great idea. But where do you think she would have made the chocolates?"

"I think the store is too small for her to be able to do it there, plus we don't have much chance of getting past that security. I think we should check her house."

"Aren't Myrtle's kids staying there?"

"Yes, and I'm sure I can get invited inside with a little convincing. Then I can take a look around her house and see if I find anything."

"All right, that's not even breaking and entering, Luke shouldn't get upset about that."

"No, he shouldn't." Ally smiled proudly. "So, it's a perfectly good way to help him solve the case."

"Sure." Charlotte's sly smile was lost behind her cup of coffee.

Chapter Thirteen

Charlotte knew where Stephanie lived, however they still parked a few streets away. Ally was sure that if Stephanie spotted her she would do her best to prevent Ally from getting inside the house. The best chance she had of getting inside was to get the attention of one of Myrtle's children. If she could get invited in by them, then she might be able to look around before Stephanie asked her to leave. When they walked up to the house Charlotte held a bouquet of flowers in front of her. Ally knocked on the door and took a slight step back. A moment later the door swung open.

"Hi Mark." Ally offered a tight smile. "My grandmother and I wanted to offer our sympathy."

"Did you?" He nodded and took the flowers from Charlotte. "Thank you."

"Could we maybe come inside for a minute?" Charlotte asked sweetly. "We feel awful about what's happened, and the fact that someone is trying to make it look like we were involved. We'd love to talk to you and your sister about what we know about the investigation, so that we can get you up to speed."

"All right, but just for a few minutes. My aunt is down at her store and she doesn't like visitors."

"Is your father here?" Charlotte stepped in front of Ally and through the door into Stephanie's house.

"No, he doesn't fly in until tomorrow."

"Fly? Does he live far?" Ally asked. She tried to keep her voice level as she followed her grandmother into the house. She had heard Nate talking to Stephanie, why would Mark believe he was out of town? Was Nate trying to hide the fact that he was in the area from his kids?

"No, but he was away on a business trip. He actually lives about twenty minutes from here. He bought himself a nice split-level place. I guess he's trying to get back on his feet."

“Back on his feet?”

Mark led them into a tidy living room. “Yes, after the divorce he took it pretty hard, and he was basically living in squalor for a long time. Motels, tiny apartments, even my aunt’s basement.”

Ally’s eyes widened. She glanced over at Charlotte who offered a subtle nod. If Stephanie and Nate had spent time living together that was likely when the romance started.

“Please, sit.” He gestured to an overstuffed, white couch. “I’d like to hear what you know.”

“Do you mind if I use the bathroom first?” Ally paused in the entrance of the living room.

“Sure. Down the hall, to the right.”

“Thanks.”

“I’ll fill you in.” Charlotte sat down on the couch and waited for Mark to take a seat as well. Ally could hear them talking as she headed down the hall. Her heart pounded. The search would not be easy. There was a good chance that Stephanie could walk in at any time, or that Mark’s sister would pop out of one of the rooms. She had to be very careful.

Ally peeked into the kitchen. It was cramped, with very cluttered counters. There wasn't a reasonable workspace. The floors were clean with no sign of chocolate footprints or smudges. She quickly opened the cupboard and then the fridge, but found nothing incriminating inside. When she closed the fridge door she noticed a door in the kitchen that she assumed led to the basement.

After a quick glance around to make sure that no one was watching, she opened the door. The stairs were wooden and rickety. She had to close the door behind her to muffle the creaks of the wood as she made her way down the steps. She envisioned a secret lab of sorts, with beakers and bubbling poison. What she found was quite different. Mountains of boxes were piled from floor to ceiling. Even if Stephanie wanted to, Ally didn't see how she could have ever made the chocolates there.

Ally made her way back to the top of the steps.

Her nerves were alive with fear as she opened the door to the kitchen. Luckily, no one was waiting for her. She closed the door quietly, then stepped into the hallway. There were four doors, two on the left, one on the right, and one at the end of the hall. Her instincts told her that the door at the end of the hall led to the master bedroom. Maybe there would be evidence of Stephanie's chocolate making in there.

With silent steps she crept her way down the hall. When she reached the room she turned the knob on the door and eased it open very carefully. On the other side was what she would expect to find in any bedroom. She quickly cast her eyes around the room, but she again found no evidence of chocolate making. Ally backed out of the room and started to turn down the hallway when she heard her grandmother clear her throat. A signal that she needed to hurry. Ally rushed to the bathroom door, which she had never even opened. She just made it when Mark walked down the hall.

“Oh sorry, was just checking on you. I thought maybe you were out of toilet paper or something.”

“No, no, it was fine. I’m sorry. I just ate something a little funny.” As soon as the words were out of her mouth she realized how awkward that statement sounded. Mark’s eyes widened, but he was polite enough not to comment. Ally felt disheartened as she joined her grandmother in the living room. Not only had she not found anything, but now she had reminded Mark that they were the ones accused of poisoning his mother.

“Well, thanks for sharing the information with me. I sure hope they find out the truth soon. My mother’s will is going to be read after the funeral. I’d like to know who her killer is before then.”

“So would we.” Charlotte stood up from the couch. “We’re going to keep you posted.”

“Thanks. That’s more than the detective on the case is doing.”

“I’m sure that the detective is working very

hard on the case and that's why he hasn't been able to keep you informed," Ally said as she stood up.

"I hope so. I really want this solved." Mark walked them both to the door. Just as he opened it, Stephanie reached for the knob. Ally nearly walked right into her.

"You two? What are you doing in my house? Mark! Did you let them in here?"

Mark shied back from his aunt's raised voice. "They were just updating me on the case, Aunt Stephanie."

"Updating you on the case? About what? How they plan to poison me next?"

"Aunt Steph, I don't think that's going to happen."

"No Mark, you don't think at all, do you?" She looked from him to Ally. "Get out of my house. And for that matter, stay away from my store as well. I want nothing to do with either of you. Don't think I won't be calling the detective about this.

You can't continue to harass us."

"It was just a visit to express our sympathy." Charlotte straightened her shoulders. "Really Stephanie, we had nothing to do with this, there's no reason to be rude."

"Sure, no reason, except that your chocolates killed my sister."

Charlotte shook her head and guided Ally out through the door. Stephanie slammed the door shut behind them. Ally instantly had a knot in her stomach. Their presence at Stephanie's house might only make them look worse.

"Mee-Maw, I didn't find anything." Ally shook her head. "I think I just blew our last chance."

"It was a long shot to begin with."

"I know. Stephanie is too smart to create the murder weapon in her own house. She must have done it somewhere else. Now Stephanie is going to call Luke," Ally said.

"That's all right, we didn't do anything wrong. We paid a visit to show our sympathy, that's all."

They settled into the car and Ally turned the key. The moment the engine revved, her eyes widened.

"Wait. Wait a minute." Ally sat forward in her seat. "I bet I know where the chocolates were made." Ally's phone rang. She saw it was Luke.

"Ally. I just got a call from Stephanie..." Luke said before she could say anything.

"Can we talk about that later? I need the address for Myrtle's ex-husband, Nate, please?"

"What? Why? Ally, we need to talk about why you were at Stephanie's."

"Okay, and I promise we will. Just not right now. Right now I need Nate's address. Please Luke?"

"Ally, I feel like you're not grasping the severity of this situation."

"I do know that this is serious and that's why I need the address?"

"No, I won't give it to you."

"I need to know his address," Ally repeated. "There's a good reason, I promise, and it's nothing

I couldn't find with an internet search, I just don't have time for that when I know that you have his address in a file right in front of you."

"Sorry, Ally I won't. You need to stay..."

"Stay out of this, I know, I know." Ally hung up the phone.

"You think they were made at Nate's house? If they were he must have been in on it." Charlotte narrowed her eyes. "Ex-wife or not, Myrtle was the mother of his children, who could be so cruel?"

"If I'm wrong then we are going to find out."

Ally searched the internet on her phone for Nate's address. The address was in Mainbry. She barely ever went to that area, but the address rang a bell. It was like she had seen it somewhere recently, but she didn't know where. "We're about to find out." She set up a map to the address. "I just need to get out onto the main road, and then we will see what we find."

***

The twenty minute drive was turned into thirty minutes because of the traffic. Ally tried not to complain, but she was getting more frustrated by the moment. She knew that every minute that ticked by was more time for Stephanie to alert Nate that they were suspicious. If Nate had the chance to clear out his house they might end up with nothing to show for their search, yet again.

"Here we are." She pulled up to a split-level house, just as Mark had described. "This is it." She double-checked the address to be sure.

"There's no car in the driveway. I don't think he's home." Charlotte leaned forward to peer through the window.

"I'll take a quick look around just to be sure. I want to see if there's any way to get into the house."

"Ally, remember what Luke said."

"I remember, but that doesn't mean that I'm not going to see what I can see. This is the best thing I can do for us right now."

"Right, but if Nate catches us we're going to have a real problem. We're out of town now, and Luke won't be able to do much to protect you if you get caught breaking in."

"I know." Ally sighed solemnly. "But I still have to try." She opened the car door and walked towards the house from the side. Just because there was no car there didn't mean that no one was home. With caution she slid along the side of the house. The bottom floor had a few windows that she could easily look through.

The interior of the house was neat, but bare, only the essential furniture and not much decoration. There was no evidence of any chocolate making that might have taken place. She peered through another window and saw straight into the kitchen. The sink was clean, the table was clear, and the counters were empty. It didn't seem as if Nate did a lot of living in the house, which made sense since Mark mentioned that his father traveled for business. She stared for some time at the kitchen in the hopes that she would find some evidence of candy creation.

No matter how long she stared she couldn't invent evidence that wasn't there. There wasn't much more that she could see on the bottom floor of the house. She glanced up at the top floor. There wasn't an easy way to climb to access the windows. She doubted that the upstairs would be much different. As she walked around the house she thought about breaking in. She didn't even know if she would be able to and she knew that it was a huge risk, but leaving there with nothing seemed like an even bigger risk. She decided to check the garage to see if there might be an entrance that she could use.

When she reached the garage she found a closed door. The door was solid with no window in it. She wiggled the doorknob. The door was locked, but when she pulled her hand away, her palm was smudged with something dark. Her heart raced as she lifted her palm to her nose. She breathed a scent that she would know anywhere, the scent of chocolate. Her eyes widened. She was sure that this must be where the chocolate was made. The windows were a few feet too high for her to see through. She looked around for something that she could stand on, but there was nothing to be found. Nate kept the outside of his house as neat and bare as the inside.

Ally's instincts and now the evidence told her that this was the place. Her heart rate quickened at the thought of walking away without confirming her instincts with proof. She needed something to stand on to see through the windows. She looked around for something to stand on but she couldn't see anything. As she walked back to the car she knew that she couldn't leave without seeing what was inside the garage. She knocked on her grandmother's window. Charlotte rolled it down.

"Did you find something?"

"I think so. But I need your help."

"Sure." Charlotte nodded. "What can I do?"

"Can you drive the car close to the garage?" she asked. "I need to stand on the hood so I can see inside."

"I can do that," Charlotte said as she walked around to the driver's side. She started the car. She slowly drove forward while Ally directed her. Ally kept indicating that she should keep moving forwards and held her hand up to stop just before the garage.

Ally gestured for Charlotte to get out and she held her grandmother's hand to steady herself as she climbed onto the hood.

"Be careful," Charlotte warned. Ally slowly climbed onto the hood. She tried to stand near the edge so she wouldn't dent it. Still holding her grandmother's hand she leaned herself against the wall to keep steady.

With her free hand Ally carefully took her phone out of her pocket so she could take photos. Once she was standing upright she could easily see in through the window.

"I can see, Mee-Maw."

"What's in there?"

“It’s mostly empty.” She peered through the dingy window and scanned the garage. “Wait, there’s a work bench. It looks like someone has been using it. What’s that?” She leaned her face closer to the window.

“What do you see?”

“Oh wow, this is the place! I see a bottle of antifreeze. I also see what looks like a small drinks fridge. Oh, and what looks like plastic molds and a camp stove. They could have been used to make the chocolates.”

“Absolutely.”

“I’m going to try to get some pictures. But the window is pretty dirty.” Ally tried to take a few pictures.

When she had finished Ally slowly crouched down on the car then stepped off with Charlotte’s help.

“I think you definitely found the place, Ally.”

“The question is, were they in on it together or was it just Nate?”

"Maybe Nate did it all alone. Maybe he poisoned the chocolates so that he could finally be free of his ex. Maybe he stood to benefit from the old will. He might have been in it still. Myrtle divorced him so he wouldn't be burdened by her when she thought she was dying, but maybe she never changed the will when they got divorced if she had no animosity towards him."

"That's a good point. And Mark said his father was still on a business trip when he clearly wasn't." Ally nodded.

"Let me see the pictures."

"I did the best I could." Ally handed the phone over to Charlotte. Charlotte flipped through the pictures and frowned.

"They're a little blurry, but I think they will do."

"I'll text them to Luke to have a look at. Maybe it will be enough to make him investigate Nate further."

"We did it, Ally. We got him!" Charlotte

exclaimed joyfully.

"Maybe." Ally frowned as she sent the texts.

"What is it?"

"I don't know. Something doesn't feel right to me," Ally said.

By the time they were both settled in the car Ally's phone began to ring. She picked it up as soon as she saw it was Luke.

"Hi Luke."

"Hi Ally. Where did you get these pictures?"

"At Nate's house. In his garage."

"Wait, in?"

"Well no, through the window."

"You were there?"

"We're still here."

"Ally."

"Luke, I sent you the pictures. You can do with them what you will. You wanted proof, I think that's pretty good proof."

“But he has an alibi.” He lowered his voice. “We ruled him out a long time ago.”

“That doesn’t mean that he wasn’t involved somehow. All I know is that the pictures are of his garage. It’s pretty clear that he was up to something.”

“I’ll look into it.”

“Can you let me know what comes of it?” Ally asked hopefully.

“I’ll try.”

“Thanks, Luke.”

“Let’s hope this leads somewhere.” He hung up the phone. Ally smiled a little to herself. She felt like she was finally getting somewhere and hopefully she and Luke wouldn’t have the murder hanging over their heads for much longer.

“He said he’ll look into it.” She glanced over at her grandmother as she started the car. “Maybe we’re finally getting somewhere.”

“Let’s hope so, sweetheart, let’s hope so.” She patted Ally’s knee as Ally reversed the car away from the garage and drove off down the street.

Chapter Fourteen

When Ally and Charlotte arrived at the cottage Ally had a strange sensation in the pit of her stomach. At first she thought it was about the case, and the photographs that she had sent to Luke. After stepping inside, Arnold raced to the door to greet them. That's when it hit Ally. There was no meow from a distant room, no pitter patter of little paws.

"Mee-Maw, have you seen Peaches?"

"Not since this morning."

Ally grimaced. "She must be hiding."

"Well, it's just about dinner time, so I'm sure if we bring her food out she will come running." Charlotte walked over to the cabinet that held the cat and pig food. When she pulled out a can of cat food and popped open the lid, they both waited for Peaches to come running. Instead they were greeted by Arnold's snorting and squealing. There was no sign of Peaches.

"Maybe she's stuck in my room. I usually leave the door open, but things were a bit strange this morning." She walked down the hall to find her bedroom door open. As was her grandmother's. Even the bathroom door stood ajar. Ally began to panic. "Peaches?" She called to the cat and snapped her fingers. That usually got her attention no matter where she was hiding. This time, no cat appeared. Breathless, Ally rushed back into the kitchen. "Mee-Maw, I can't find her. Did she come in here?"

"No, I haven't seen her." Charlotte frowned. "Do you think it's possible she slipped out the door?"

"She does have a track record of escaping." Ally suddenly gasped. "I don't think I closed the door tightly earlier today when Luke brought Arnold. I bet she got out then."

"Oh, Ally, I'm sure she'll be fine. It's not like she hasn't gone exploring before and she always comes back."

"She usually only goes out for an hour or two,

but I think she's been out on her own for almost an entire day. How am I going to find her?"

"It's good weather, and she knows her way home, Ally. I know why you're worried, but she will come home."

Ally looked out the window at the fading sunlight. Her eyes squinted into the growing shadows.

"I hope she comes home before it's too dark."

"Let's have some dinner, then we can go out looking if she hasn't come home."

"Okay." Ally sighed. She assisted her grandmother in preparing a meal, but her heart ached with worry. She wanted Peaches back with her, where she knew that she was safe. When she saw Luke's car pull up out front she hoped that he might have Peaches. After all, just that morning he had brought Arnold home. However, when he stepped out of the car he walked straight to the door with no cat in his hands. She waited for him to knock then she opened the door.

"Luke?"

"Hi, I wanted to be the first to tell you the good news."

Ally was so worried about Peaches that it was hard for her to believe that there was anything that could be good news.

"What is it?"

"You and your grandmother can reopen the shop."

"Really?" Ally's eyes widened. "That is good news. But why?"

"We found nothing incriminating at the shop and we have a main suspect, thanks to you."

"Do you mean, Nate?"

"Yes, I looked through the delivery records and there wasn't a delivery to Freely Lakes on the day of Myrtle's murder, but Nate used his credit card to order a box of chocolates and have them delivered to his house from your shop the day before Myrtle's murder." Suddenly Ally remembered why Nate's address was familiar to her, she had seen it entered in the GPS in the van. "He came home early from his work trip so his alibi wasn't a hundred percent solid. We served a search warrant on his house. We found the evidence that you photographed now we are just waiting for his arrest warrant to come through. "

"That's great." Ally sighed.

"You don't seem too happy."

"I am happy." Ally smiled. "I can't wait to tell Mee-Maw."

"What's wrong?" Luke caught her elbow. "Talk to me, Ally. Did something happen?"

Ally tried not to let her worry show, but it was impossible to hide the crease in her brow. "Peaches got out this morning I guess. I don't know where she is."

"Oh, I'm sorry, Ally. I'll keep an eye out for her, okay?"

Ally nodded. "Thanks, Luke. And I am really happy about the store reopening."

"I know you are. Just do me a favor and take

it easy, all right?"

"Take it easy?"

"I mean, there's going to be a lot of heat on the shop still. Just be careful until we get all of this settled."

"I will. Do you want to come in and tell Mee-Maw yourself?"

"No, I think I'd better go. I don't know when the arrest warrant will be signed."

"I hope it's soon. Myrtle's funeral is tomorrow."

"I know." Luke frowned gravely. "I want all of this to be settled before then, trust me."

"If there's anything I can do..."

"You've done plenty, Ally. Really you have."

"And so have you, Luke. I appreciate what you've done."

"I've done what I could, and will continue to do so. Just remember things can change. Don't let your guard down." He met her eyes. "Keep a low profile until an official arrest has been made."

"I can do that," Ally said. "I am going to be spending my time looking for Peaches anyway."

"All right." He grasped her hand briefly, then released it. "Good night, Ally."

"Night, Luke." Despite her concern for Peaches she couldn't help but smile. As soon as he was back in his car Ally stepped into the cottage. "Mee-Maw, guess what?"

"What?" Charlotte wiped her hands on her apron as she met Ally in the hall.

"Luke said we can reopen the shop."

"Oh, that's wonderful! We'll open tomorrow! Oh no, wait." She shook her head. "I don't think that would be a good idea."

"No?"

"Well, the funeral is tomorrow, I think it might be disrespectful to do that."

"You're right, we can wait to open."

"At least we got the green light."

"I wish I could go to the funeral to pay my respects."

"Me too," Charlotte said. "But I don't think we should, seeing as common belief is that our chocolates killed Myrtle."

"I know," Ally agreed. "What about Peaches? I think I should go look for her."

"I think you should wait till tomorrow. Put a dish of her food outside. I'm sure that she will be back by the morning. You know that she likes to wander sometimes. Try not to worry."

"I'm trying not to worry." Ally put some food in a dish and placed it outside. The entire time she hoped that Peaches would come running up to her. However, there was no cat to be seen. Ally went to bed that night with her heart aching. Though she tried to sleep, she could barely close her eyes without thinking of Peaches and where she might be. It wasn't normal to lose two pets in such a short span of time, but she had. She should have felt relieved that the shop was going to be reopened, but instead she was faced with the horrible thought of what might have happened to Peaches.

Chapter Fifteen

Ally woke with a start the next morning. She jumped out of bed, raced down the hall, and out onto the front porch. There sat Peaches' bowl, with her food untouched. Tears rushed to Ally's eyes.

"Ally sweetheart, it's going to be okay." Charlotte walked up behind her and put an arm around her shoulders. "She will come home, and she will be fine. We'll go looking for her, okay?"

"Yes. I want to go right now." She hurried back into the house, changed as fast as she could and was ready to walk right back out the door.

"Wait a minute." Her grandmother stood between her and the door. "You need to have some coffee first, and something to eat. It's only going to make it more difficult to find Peaches on an empty stomach."

"No way. How can I eat when I don't even know if she has food?"

"Ally, Peaches always finds her way to food. People in town know to look out for her. It's going to be okay. But if you try to go out looking for her now you're just going to get tired in a few minutes. It's really important that you keep your strength."

"I know you're right, I just feel so awful about it."

"Come and sit with me. It feels like months since we've been able to relax about the shop, even though it's only been a few days. I really want us to be able to reopen the shop on a positive note."

"Me too." Ally slumped down into one of the kitchen chairs. "I just don't know how quickly the community is going to be able to forget our involvement, even with a suspect in custody."

"It will take some time, I know that." Charlotte set coffee down for both of them along with some pastries. "I have to say I'm really impressed with how you figured it all out."

"I'm not sure that I did figure it all out."

"Isn't Luke arresting Nate?"

"Yes, I think he is. But the problem is I'm not convinced it was Nate."

"Love can make you do the wildest things." Charlotte took a long swallow of her coffee. "The question is, was it love? Was it hate? Was it purely financial? It could have been a wide variety of things."

"Yes, you're right," Ally agreed. "I can't even think clearly with Peaches missing."

"Well, finish up and we'll go out and look together."

"No Mee-Maw, I know that you have your packing to do. I can go look by myself. It will be okay," Ally said. "Besides, if you're here you can call me if Peaches comes home."

"If you insist that's fine. Your instincts are probably better for finding her, anyway." She polished off her pastry. "Maybe Luke could take you for a ride around town."

"I don't think so. I imagine he's very busy."

"I doubt that he would be too busy for you, if

you asked."

Ally lowered her eyes and nodded a little. "You might be right."

"But you don't like that?"

"I do, it's just on the one hand there's this huge sensation between us, almost like a pull, but on the other hand it feels like there is always this barrier."

"It must be hard to even consider trusting again, Ally." Charlotte looked at her with warmth and understanding.

"It is." Ally took the last bite of her pastry.

"It's important to remember that just because one man wasn't worthy of your trust, that doesn't mean that none of them will be."

"I know you're right, Mee-Maw, but I just can't seem to convince my heart of that. Every time I start to feel something, I just pull back. I'm not sure what Luke is thinking either. He just may not want to risk getting involved with me."

"Why do you think it would be a risk?"

Charlotte raised an eyebrow.

"Because, I'm always getting in the middle of things. Maybe I'm too involved in the community. Maybe he just wants to focus on his career." Ally shrugged. "I can't sort it out right now."

"If not now, then when?" Charlotte met her eyes. "I think it's time that you stopped avoiding what you really want. If it's not Luke, that's fine, but you need to figure it out. I've never seen a man more head-over-heels."

"Mee-Maw, I think you're exaggerating." Ally stood up to clear the dishes. Her grandmother's soft voice wafted towards her.

"Ally, he has a heart, too, you know." Ally froze in front of the sink. Of course she knew that Luke had feelings, but she hadn't really considered whether she might be hurting him. Her main concern had been about protecting herself from harm. Yet, she had encouraged his attention every step of the way without much thought to the consequences that he might face as a result. She bit into her bottom lip as she turned to face her grandmother.

"Do you see? What am I going to do with myself without you here to guide me?"

"I'll only be a few minutes away, Ally, remember?"

Ally nodded. "I'm going to go look for Peaches."

"Okay, sweetie. Good luck."

"Thanks." Ally was determined not to return to the cottage without Peaches.

***

Ally decided to walk, since that would be the best way to spot Peaches. As she walked along the sidewalk into town she noticed that there were very few people outside. She looked up at the sky. Thick, black clouds billowed above her. Right away she regretted making the decision to walk. But instead of turning back she continued forward. She didn't want Peaches to be stuck out in the rain. The closer to town she got, the heavier the clouds became.

Ally checked the deli where Peaches would sometimes find some scraps when she got out. She wanted to ask the owner if she had seen her, but the deli was closed. There was a small sign on the door that listed an opening time of one in the afternoon. Ally assumed that the owner planned to attend the funeral.

As she expected, the convenience store was closed. There weren't many places that were open. Above her the sky rumbled. Ally sighed as she leaned against the wall of the pharmacy. The rain began to spatter against the sidewalk. Ally hoped that maybe the rain would drive Peaches back to the cottage. As she started to walk back towards the cottage, a car pulled up beside her. Ally couldn't recognize it through the much heavier rain that had begun to fall.

"Ally, what are you doing out in this mess?" Luke leaned out of the window to look at her. "Get in the car."

Ally walked around to the passenger side and slid inside. "Sorry, I think I got your seat wet."

"I'm not worried about that. Why are you out here?"

"I was looking for Peaches."

"She hasn't come home yet?" Luke looked over at her. "You must be worried sick."

"I am." Ally was glad that her cheeks were already damp from the rain as a few tears escaped. She had never been so worried about Peaches before. The cat was her best friend and the one good thing that had come out of her marriage.

"Hey, we're going to find her." Luke reached over and rubbed his hand over the back of hers. She shivered a little from the touch. "Are you cold? Of course you are. You're soaked from the rain." He shuffled out of his jacket. Once it was off he draped it around her shoulders. Then he reached for his radio. As Ally listened, a detective, who had many more important cases, asked all patrol officers to be on the lookout for Peaches.

"Thank you so much." Ally smiled at him. "That means a lot to me."

"I know how much you care about your cat. I've seen how much you love her, Ally. I want to make sure she is safe, too." He reached out and wrapped an arm around her shoulders. The moment he did a wave of tears washed over her. She turned into his shoulder and rested her head against him. His fingertips trailed down through her hair. The motion calmed her to the very core. "She's going to come home to you, Ally, she loves you, too." His voice caught in his throat as if he might have something else to say. The car filled with silence until he offered Ally a tissue. Ally accepted it and pulled away from him. Her cheeks burned as she looked out the window. Had she really just flung herself against Luke? She didn't dare look in his direction. The engine roared to life and Luke began to drive slowly down the road.

"She probably found shelter in all of this. Don't worry, the storm is going to pass quickly."

Ally did her best to change the subject. "Did you arrest Nate yet?"

"No, still waiting on a signature." Luke shook

his head. "Sometimes I have no idea what the powers that be are up to."

Ally nodded. "It must be tough to have your every move questioned."

"Tougher when you're the one asking the questions." Luke flashed a grin at her. Ally managed a smile in return.

"I'm not that bad."

"Oh?" He leaned a little closer to her, but kept his eyes on the road. "I guess we'll have to agree to disagree because you certainly keep me honest. I appreciate that about you, Ally, that you're not afraid to say what you're thinking, and demand honesty from others. That's a really good quality and hard to find."

"Oh Luke, I do believe you're flattering me." She cast him a wink.

"It's the truth, Ally." He stopped the car in the driveway of the cottage. She started to open the door, but he caught her hand before she could. "I don't know if I've made it clear enough to you,

Ally, but I care about you. If you need help looking for Peaches when the rain clears, call me. I'll help you. All right?"

Ally met his eyes as her cheeks heated up once more. "Thanks Luke," she said as she handed him back his jacket.

He gave her hand a squeeze and then released it. Ally opened the car door and ran through the rain to the front door of the cottage. Her heart jumped into her throat as she hoped that maybe Peaches had returned home because of the rain.

"Mee-Maw, is she home?"

Charlotte stepped into the kitchen and shook her head. "I'm sorry, Ally. Not yet."

Ally's heart sunk. "I'm going to get changed and go check around town again. The funeral should be over soon so I can maybe ask at some of the shops."

"All right, sweetheart." Ally noticed that for the first time Charlotte wore a worried frown.

Chapter Sixteen

Ally decided to drive into town. The rain had cleared up, but the sky was still heavy and gray. The grass was slick as Ally walked across it to her car. When she reached the center of town Ally parked her car and got out. There was a large crowd clustered together at the end of the street, all in dark clothing, some with umbrellas hoisted above their heads. She presumed that the funeral had just finished.

She turned to walk down the street. She saw some patrol cars drive past her and she turned to see them pull up at the parking area she was walking away from. When she saw Luke, along with a few other officers, get out of the cars and turn in her direction she ducked behind a tree. Were they there to arrest her? Had Luke's influence finally run out? Ally's heart raced as they walked closer and closer to her. She clenched her jaw and gripped the tree. It flashed through her mind that maybe if she held on tight enough they wouldn't be able to arrest her. As she waited for the arrival of the officers she was stunned when they continued past her, further into the group.

"Excuse me." Luke paused at the back of the crowd.

The crowd began to murmur and they parted to allow the officers past. For the first time Ally saw that Nate was at the back of the crowd. She hadn't even noticed him there. Stephanie along with Nate's two children stood close to him. Ally watched Luke's broad shoulders straighten as he walked up to Nate. Nate looked back at him with annoyance.

"Is this really necessary? We've just been at a funeral."

"It is very necessary. You're under arrest for the murder of your ex-wife, Myrtle Dents. We can do this quietly, or we can forcibly detain you."

"What?" Nate stared at him with wide eyes. "This can't be happening." He looked over at his children who stood close to Stephanie. "It's not true, I promise you it's not true. I would never hurt your mother." Neither of them said a word. Stephanie hugged them both.

"Don't worry, Nate. This is just a bunch of lies," Stephanie said.

Luke grabbed him by the elbow and pulled him away from the crowd. Nate didn't fight back. As Luke escorted him past Ally, she could see the dazed look on Nate's face. She assumed he was shocked to be caught. Nate's arrest left a flurry of whispers and gasps in his wake. Ally continued to keep herself concealed. She was relieved that she was not the one the police were there for, but her stomach twisted with guilt. Despite the evidence she had found in Nate's garage, that the police had confirmed, tearing Nate away from his family so publicly seemed wrong.

As the crowd dispersed Ally started walking around the streets looking for Peaches, but there was no sign of her. Most of the shops were still closed so she decided to head home, she could come back later after she had told her grandmother about Nate. As she headed for her car, she thought about the way Nate looked as he was escorted away. It seemed odd to her that he was so shocked. If he had murdered Myrtle, wouldn't he have expected the possibility of being caught? Maybe he thought that he had created such a perfect crime that he never entertained the idea of being caught.

***

At the cottage Charlotte had lunch waiting for Ally.

"Thanks Mee-Maw, but I don't know if I can eat."

"Worried about Peaches?"

"Yes. And Luke arrested Nate."

"Where, at the service?" Charlotte's eyes widened.

"No, I saw Luke arrest him in town after the service," Ally explained.

"Oh boy, I bet the entire town is going to be talking about that."

“I think so, too.”

“So, what’s wrong, Ally? You should be happy that he was arrested.”

“I don’t know. I just can’t shake this feeling that something is wrong with all of this. I am also so worried about Peaches.”

Charlotte gave her a warm hug. “Why don’t we pack up lunch and take it with us to the shop? I’ve arranged for some ingredients to be delivered this afternoon and with the arrest people might be ready to come back to the shop. We can get everything prepared for opening tomorrow. That might be a good way to get your mind off things.”

“Yes, it might.” Ally nodded. “Just give me a minute.” She just needed a minute to steady her nerves and gather her thoughts.

“Sure, I’ll pack up. We can get some more supplies from the grocery store on the way.”

Ally stepped into her bedroom and was immediately struck by the fact that Peaches wasn’t there. Her room felt so empty without her.

It was impossible to think of that being a permanent feeling. Had someone else found her and taken her in? Most people in town knew that Peaches was her cat. But maybe someone from out of town had come across her. Ally took a few deep breaths to calm down, but she couldn't, she was fraught with worry.

***

When Ally and Charlotte arrived at the shop Ally took a few minutes to call all the shelters in the area. None had a cat meeting Peaches' description. She decided she would go check them anyway the next day.

"I'll go door to door and ask if anyone's seen her. I need to let everyone know we're reopening anyway," Charlotte said.

"Are you sure, Mee-Maw? They might not be too happy about it."

"That's fine, they don't need to be happy, they just need to know, so they can keep their gossiping to a minimum."

Ally nodded. She cleaned the counters and the floors while her grandmother was gone. Her thoughts returned to the chocolate on Stephanie's shoe. Was it just a coincidence? Was she in on it with Nate? When Charlotte returned Ally looked up at her with hope.

"I'm sorry, Ally, no one has seen her, but they all promised to look for her around their stores."

"How were they about the shop reopening?"

"Surprisingly warm. Most of the other store owners are very happy about it, and a lot showed us both support."

"Well, that's something." Ally smiled.

"Yes, it is." Charlotte sighed with relief. "Ally, we have nothing to sell. Do you want to make a batch of chocolates with me?"

"I don't know. Even if the other shop owners are happy for us, that doesn't mean we'll have customers."

"But what if we do?" Charlotte smiled. "Then they will have fresh chocolates and beautiful smells filling the store. Besides, we have to have something to sell them if they come in."

"I guess." Ally swallowed back her concern as she followed her grandmother into the kitchen. "I'm ready to get my mind off things, if that is possible. I'm sorry for being so negative."

"Ally, I know why you're worried, you love Peaches. Let's try focusing on the positives of our situation. At least there is a suspect in custody."

"I have to be honest, I don't think it was him."

"Maybe not, but you are now in a position where you have no control over the case. They have their suspect, and it's up to Luke to figure out the truth."

"Maybe, I just have a hard time seeing Stephanie as being innocent in all of this. I mean she must have played a part."

"Or maybe you're a little jaded by your own past and expect that to be the case?"

"Maybe." Ally shrugged. She watched as her grandmother gathered the ingredients for the chocolates she wanted to create. “I just can’t shake this sensation that we are missing something.”

“Maybe once Peaches comes back that feeling will subside. You have a lot of emotions running through that heart of yours right now, Ally.”

“Not only that, but I am thinking about my best friend leaving,” Ally said as Charlotte turned to face her with a broad smile.

“Aw, I love you too, sweetie. I will only be a few minutes away.” Charlotte handed her a spoon to stir the melted chocolate.

“I know. And I am sure you will have a great time at Freely Lakes.”

“I think so, too. I love all of the options of activities that I will get to enjoy.”

“I’m sure that you will have a blast.” Ally smiled at her as she began pouring the chocolate into the molds.

“It will never be as much fun as making chocolates with you.”

"Aw!" Ally grinned at her. The bell above the door rang as it swung open. "Oh, did we leave the front door open? I'll go see who it is." Charlotte nodded. Ally walked from the back room into the front. "Sorry, we're closed."

Luke turned towards her. His eyes met hers. "You don't have to worry about being a suspect anymore, Ally."

Ally's cheeks flushed the moment she laid eyes on him. "Why?"

"Well, Nate confessed."

"What?" Ally's eyes widened. "Are you sure?"

"Yes, I took his confession myself." Luke shoved his hands into his pockets. "He said all of the right things. He said he did everything himself and that Stephanie had nothing to do with it. He wanted Myrtle dead before she changed her will." She studied him.

"But you don't believe him, do you?" Ally asked.

"I have no reason not to. The case is going to

be closed as soon as the paperwork is filed. Myrtle's will is going to be read and all of this will be settled. It's over, Ally. It's finally over." He rocked back on his heels.

"Luke, why don't you think it was him?" Ally asked, persisting with what she believed was on Luke's mind.

"I didn't say that I don't." He lowered his chin and shifted his gaze towards the wooden sculptures that lined the shelves.

"You don't have to say it. I can tell."

"So, now you know more about me than I do?" He raised an eyebrow.

"You can trust me, Luke. You know that, don't you?"

"Do you trust me?" He folded his arms across his chest. Ally's voice faltered. She wasn't sure how to answer him. She had trusted a man once, and it had led to heartbreak. Luke spoke through her silence. "So, if you don't trust me, how can you expect me to know that I can trust you?"

"I think I've shown that you can," Ally said.

"By going to Nate's house? By following Stephanie? Let's not forget about breaking into Myrtle's room?"

"I did what I thought was right."

"What you did was put yourself in danger, despite my warnings." He unfolded his arms and met her eyes again. "Ally, you're reckless, you're going to get hurt. I've tried to make it clear to you the amount of danger that you put yourself in, but you don't seem to be able to grasp it."

"What, so I'm not allowed to be brave and try to clear my grandmother's name."

He reached out and caught her hand with his own. Ally was startled by the touch, but she didn't pull away. "Or maybe, you could rely on me a little more."

Ally's cheeks heated up. "I will try."

"Good." He released her hand, then glanced around the shop. "I guess I should let you open up."

"You don't seem too happy about it."

"I'm not, to be honest. I'm very concerned. I'm not convinced that Nate is the killer, even with his confession. I'm worried that someone will take advantage of the shop being back open, and poison more chocolates. I just hope that you and your grandmother take that into consideration before you open for business."

"We will, and we'll be careful," Ally promised him.

"Good." He nodded. "If you need anything, just call me." He turned and walked out of the shop.

Now that Ally knew that Luke was not happy about the shop reopening, she wondered who he thought the real killer might be.

Chapter Seventeen

Ally and Charlotte had just finished up the batch of chocolates when Ally's phone began ringing. She saw that it was Luke and picked it up right away.

"Hello?"

"Hey Ally, I just wanted to let you know that someone called in a tip about Peaches being near the convenience store."

"Oh wow! Thanks Luke!" She hung up before he could say another word.

"Mee-Maw, Peaches was seen near the convenience store. I'm going to look!"

"I'll go grab Arnold and we'll look, too. I'm sure he can sniff her out if she's nearby." Charlotte clapped her hands happily. The two rushed out of the shop in different directions.

When Ally got to the convenience store she looked all around, but she didn't find Peaches. "Maybe she ran off somewhere," she said to herself. She continued down the street behind the store. There were a few more buildings there including a vacant shop.

"Peaches, here kitty kitty!" Ally rounded the corner of the empty building. It was darker than she expected on the other side. "Peaches, come here, sweetie. I know you've got to be hungry. Peaches!" Ally's heartbeat quickened. Maybe she was afraid that she wouldn't find her cat. But all of the hairs on the back of her neck stood up. She searched the shadows for any sign of her cat. Her heart ached for her dearest friend. "Peaches, please come home, I miss you." She sighed and walked behind a large dumpster to see if maybe the cat was hiding.

As soon as she walked behind the dumpster she noticed a big wooden gate that blocked her way forward. The splintered wood highlighted by a distant streetlight made her feel very uneasy. She spun around fast to walk away, but found Stephanie standing in front of her. Ally gasped.

"I'm sorry, I didn't mean to scare you,"

Stephanie said.

"It's okay." Ally placed her hand on her chest. "I just didn't expect anyone to be behind me."

"I heard you calling for your cat. I thought you might want some help looking for her."

"Oh. That's nice of you."

Stephanie stepped closer to her. "I had a cat once. It's not easy when they run away."

"I don't think she ran away." Ally frowned. "I think she's just exploring. Maybe she's just a little confused."

"That's possible. Here, let me see your phone, I can shine it behind the dumpster to see if she's back there."

Ally handed it over without thinking. She was concentrating on finding Peaches and she was still so shaken by Stephanie suddenly being there that her mind was spinning. The second she handed it to Stephanie, she regretted it. Sure, someone was arrested for the murder. But that didn't mean that they were right. Stephanie leaned over and shone the phone behind the dumpster.

"Oh, what's that?" She leaned her arm in further. "Oh no, it's nothing."

Ally heard a clatter. "What was that?"

"Oh dear, I'm afraid I dropped your phone."

"What?" Ally frowned. "Let me see, maybe I can get it."

"Sure, you do that." Stephanie stepped back from the dumpster to give Ally room. But she didn't give her much room at all. In fact, Ally was pinned between Stephanie and the dumpster. When Ally peered behind the dumpster she could see her phone in the dirt and grime. She tried to reach for it, but as she bent forward, she felt Stephanie's arm go around her waist, pinning her other arm against her side.

"What are you doing?" Ally gasped and tried to pull her other arm out from behind the dumpster, but the pressure of Stephanie's weight kept her arm wedged. "Let me go!"

"I'm afraid I can't do that, Ally. You're the

only person that can ruin my future. I need you to die. I wish I didn't, but it's the only way I can be sure that the police will stop sniffing around me."

"No, you don't have to. Please! The police already think that it's someone else."

"Sure they do. But it's the wrong someone else. It was meant to be you. I went to great lengths to make them think that you and Charlotte did this. But I know now that you won't give up. One slip up and you'd be on my back again. I've waited a long time to have the family that I deserve, and I'm not going to let you or anyone else take it from me. So unfortunately, curiosity killed the Ally. Get it, like Ally cat?" She giggled. Ally was in a state of disbelief as the woman giggled behind her. How could anyone be so cold? Then again, she had killed her own sister.

"Please Stephanie. I haven't done anything to you. You had a reason to kill Myrtle, but you don't have a reason to kill me."

"Sure I do. Just like Myrtle you are standing in the way of what I want. Nate's a good man. He had nothing to do with this. If he's not in jail for the murder then I will be. So, I've got to keep this under wraps. I've got to make sure they think it was you and that you've run away because you don't want to get caught. Now, if you're still, this will be quick." She began pushing up the sleeve of the arm that was pinned against Ally's side. Ally struggled, but she was stuck. There was no way for her to get free.

"Poisoning the chocolates was a genius move on my part, you have to admit. Plus, I must give you some credit for giving me the idea. You see, I knew that I wanted to poison her, but I didn't know how. When you bought the antifreeze it was like a light bulb went off in my head. Not only did I figure out how to poison her, but I also figured out what to poison. Because she loved your chocolates so much. She gorged herself on them, and she never shared. When I was a child she would buy herself all kinds of treats, but she would never let me have any. She would eat them right in front of me!"

"That's terrible. I'm sorry that happened to you."

"You don't know the half of it. She was terrible to me. She treated me like I was a servant. Then I met this man. I thought, this is the man for me. He will change my life. But she saw that I liked him. She swooped in and spoiled him with her riches and conned him into marrying her. She took my husband from me, before I even had the chance to tell him how I felt. By the time I did it was too late. She was pregnant with her first and he was too good of a man to ever leave her. So, I had to watch as she took my family from me. She didn't even treat the kids well. Not at all. She barely paid any attention to them. I always took over when she was too busy."

"That is awful, Stephanie, and all the more reason not to kill me. You have plenty of reason to justify killing your sister. A jury will sympathize with you. But they're not going to let you off the hook for killing me."

"Oh, that will never happen. I will never go to

trial. Your body will never be found. The poison in the candies took some time, but I'm injecting the poison right into your bloodstream. It will be quick. Then I will toss your body into the dumpster. In just a few hours the dumpster will be collected and all trace of you will be gone."

Ally's eyes blurred with fear. Now she knew why Stephanie took her phone from her. Now she knew why she had been there in the first place. She had probably even been the one to call in the tip about Peaches. She tried to calm her nerves. She wanted to distract Stephanie. Try to delay the inevitable.

"How did you get Nate to help you?" Ally asked.

"I didn't, he came back early, unannounced. I was meant to clean up the garage before he came home, but I didn't have time. Luckily he didn't go in there."

"How did you poison the chocolates?"

"That just fell into place so easily." Stephanie smirked. "The expresso, walnut chocolates are my favorite. They were Myrtle's, too. Nate knew that I liked them and he wanted to give me a gift. He had some delivered to his house for me a few days ago. I had his keys so I could let the men in to repair his heater and when I got to his house the chocolates were waiting for me, on the doorstep."

"How did you make them?"

"I tried to break into the chocolate shop to see if I could get any fillings or molds to make the poisoned chocolates, but I couldn't."

"You tampered with the lock?"

"Yes, but I couldn't get it open. So, I had to improvise. I made some chocolate molds myself. That's easy enough," Stephanie said proudly. "Then I cut some of the walnut, expresso chocolates Nate had given me and I took out as much liquid as I could. I didn't have to cut many. The antifreeze bulked it up nicely. I placed a walnut on top, put the poisoned ones back in the box and delivered them to my dear sister as a present. I couldn't believe my luck when you and your grandmother brought chocolates to Freely

Lakes on the same day that Myrtle died. When I found your lost cat I had the genius idea to keep her so I could use her as bait to get you here. I just had to wait for the right time to call in the tip. It worked out perfectly. Now, I just have to make sure it ends perfectly."

"You don't have to kill me," Ally said as she hoped that Peaches was okay. She couldn't believe how callous Stephanie was being, but she didn't want to antagonize her more.

"Oh, yes I do," Stephanie said. "Enough talking, time to get rid of you." Ally knew that this was it as Stephanie drew closer to her. Ally's eyes flooded with tears as she gave in to the fact that there was no escape. She could feel the needle prick against her skin.

"No!" Ally started to scream. She knew once the needle went in it wouldn't matter if someone found her. Her scream was drowned out by a high pitched screech. Ally looked up in time to see Peaches flying through the air. The cat landed with her claws out, on the hand that held the needle. Stephanie cursed and dropped the needle as she tried to shake the cat off. Ally was able to get free, but when she reached for the needle on the ground, Stephanie pounced on her from behind. Ally was slammed down hard against the pavement.

As pain flooded her vision she thought she heard a snort. In the next moment she felt Stephanie struggle above her. She was shoved backwards off Ally. Ally tried to jump up but was too dizzy to get her footing. She leaned heavily against the side of the dumpster. Only then did she see Stephanie. She was rolling on the ground with Charlotte. They rolled towards the needle that was still on the ground.

Ally lurched forward and tried to get the needle, but Stephanie reached for it at the same time. The needle rolled across the ground. Ally reached for it again, and Stephanie released Charlotte. Stephanie lunged for Ally. Ally was already unsteady on her feet. When Stephanie collided with her she collapsed to the ground.

Stephanie's weight pinned her down. Ally was sure that if Stephanie had the chance she would kill her. With all of her strength she pushed upward and managed to get Stephanie flipped under her.

"Hey! Break it up!" Luke got into the fray and tried to peel Ally off Stephanie.

"She's trying to kill me!"

"I'm here, Ally, I'm here. Let go, I'll take care of her."

Ally looked into his eyes briefly, then released her grip on Stephanie. She collapsed on the ground, exhausted from the fight. As she lay there Peaches walked up to her and nuzzled her cheek. Arnold snorted and pushed his nose against her forehead. Ally heard the click of handcuffs, a scuffle, and then Luke's grunt as he lifted Stephanie up from the ground.

"Let me go! Let me go!" Stephanie thrashed against his grasp.

"The only place you're going is lock-up." Luke

turned towards Ally. "Ally, Mrs. Sweet. Are you okay?" he called.

Ally forced herself to sit up. She spotted Charlotte sitting on the curb beside the empty building trying to catch her breath.

"Mee-Maw, are you okay?"

"I'm okay if you're okay."

"I'm okay." Ally blinked her eyes slowly with disbelief. "I'm okay." She cradled Peaches in her arms and stroked Arnold's ears. She felt so lucky to have so many heroes. As she watched Luke lead Stephanie to the police car she tried to stand up. Her body ached from striking the pavement. She limped her way over to the curb and plopped herself down beside her grandmother.

"Wow, that was a close call." Charlotte wiped her brow which was covered in sweat.

"Yes, it was." Ally glanced down at the tiny, red pinprick on her arm. The needle hadn't gone in far enough to deliver any of the deadly concoction, but it certainly had come close. "Are you sure you're okay?"

"Yes, just a little winded. I'm just so glad that Arnold heard you screaming. I thought I heard something, but I wasn't sure. Then Arnold started tugging and pulling so hard he nearly pulled me over."

"Peaches saved my life." Ally kissed the top of her cat's head. "And so did you, and Arnold."

"And your detective saved us all." Charlotte tipped her head in his direction as he walked back towards them. "He's a keeper," Charlotte added. Ally smiled.

"Ally, are you sure that you're okay?" Luke crouched down in front of her. "You have a bump on your head." He reached out to touch the reddened skin. Ally winced and caught his hand.

"I'm okay, I promise." She held onto his hand as he lowered it. "Thank you, Luke."

"When I saw you on the ground, I was so worried." He met her eyes. "Try not to scare me like that again, all right?"

Ally broke into a grin. "Sure, I'll remember that next time someone tries to inject me with antifreeze."

"Don't even joke about that." He frowned.

"Mrs. Sweet, are you okay? Luke asked.

"You can call me Charlotte." She smiled. "I'm fine, thank you."

"Nate said that he was covering for Stephanie. He said he had worked out what she had done. He was still at the conference on the day of the murder, but he came back early once he heard about Myrtle's murder," Luke said.

"Stephanie said that he wasn't involved. She tried to kill me because she thought I would discover the truth and she wanted me to take the fall. I really don't think that he was involved."

"How about you just take a five minute break from crime solving?" He leaned close to her. "At least long enough to get some rest."

"I guess that I could do that." She smiled.

Chapter Eighteen

Ally did exactly as Luke asked and got some rest. With Peaches nestled beside her in bed and Arnold curled up on the rug beside her bed, she slept for hours. It turned out that even the pets were too exhausted to fight with each other. When she finally woke up it was to the delicious aroma of chocolate cake. She washed her face and brushed her teeth and hair. She did it quickly because the smell was making her hungry.

Ally wandered into the kitchen.

"Mee-Maw?"

"I'm sorry if I woke you." Charlotte set the cake on the table.

"Oh wow, that looks amazing. How did you have the energy to make it?"

"When I get upset, I bake. It helps me sort things out, plus there is always a yummy treat waiting for me at the end."

"It does look yummy." Ally smiled.

"It smells yummy, too." Luke grinned as he stepped in from the hall. Ally gasped and took a step back. As usual she was in her pajamas.

"Oh, did I forget to tell you that Luke was here?" Charlotte winked at her as she poured three glasses of milk. "I thought he might like to join us for a slice of cake."

"Yes, you could have told me that." Ally frowned.

"I can go, if you like." Luke met her eyes.

"No, of course not. Please stay. Let me just go change." She started to turn away.

"You look perfect to me." Ally blushed slightly as Luke pulled out a chair for her. "I have some things to tell you about the case."

Ally was tempted, just as Luke knew she would be. She settled down in the chair just as her grandmother plopped a piece of cake on her plate. Luke sat down beside her, then Charlotte joined them as well. They were all too consumed by the delicious taste of the cake to speak to one another at first.

"Oh Mee-Maw, I think this is the best chocolate cake I have ever tasted."

"You always say that, until I make another one." Charlotte grinned.

"I mean it!" Ally laughed.

"I have to agree with Ally on this one. Thank you so much, Charlotte."

"Thank you, Luke. I know how hard you worked on this case to try and get our shop back open, and how you looked out for Ally. That means a lot to both of us."

Luke looked over at Ally and smiled. "I'm just glad that she's safe, and that you are, too, Charlotte."

"So, what happened?" Ally shook her head. "Why would Nate confess if he had nothing to do with the murder?"

"Well, as we suspected he and Stephanie had been having an affair. He was heartbroken when Myrtle left him. He worked out what Stephanie had done and when he was arrested he confessed to protect her. Stephanie on the other hand poisoned Myrtle because her sister had told her that she was changing her will to leave all of her wealth to charity. She wanted to kill her before the will was finalized."

"She wanted everything, the family and the money. Maybe she thought that if she wasn't rich like Myrtle, Nate wouldn't want to be with her," Ally suggested.

"That's possible. Or maybe she just wanted the money. I guess she knew that Nate's confession would turn out to be useless. There were several witnesses that placed him at his business conference at the time of the murder. She knew that you suspected her and she thought killing you would prevent her from becoming the next suspect. She wanted you to take the fall. She thought that way she and Nate could finally live their lives together."

"Could you imagine if those two had been able to inherit all of Myrtle's money?" Charlotte clucked her tongue. "How horrible that would have been."

"They wouldn't have either way. Myrtle's will was final. She left everything to charity," Luke said.

"Oh wow, I hope the kids weren't upset," Ally said.

"Not at all. She made sure they each had enough to comfortably sustain themselves for the rest of their lives before she ever changed her will. I think she suspected the relationship between Nate and Stephanie and wanted to make sure they didn't get their hands on the money."

"How sad." Ally sighed. "To think that a family could treat each other that way. I'm so lucky to have you, Mee-Maw."

"I'm lucky to have you too, Ally." Charlotte patted the back of her hand with a loving touch.

"It is sad." Luke nodded. "From what I understand Myrtle wasn't too kind to her sister, but that's no excuse for murder. At least now

Myrtle has her justice."

"To Myrtle." Ally lifted a forkful of chocolate cake into the air as a toast.

"To Myrtle." Charlotte lifted a forkful as well. Luke joined in with his fork high in the air. As they finished their cake, Ally was glad that the truth had finally come out.

"How are you feeling?" Luke asked as she walked him to the door.

"Better than I expected. I thought I'd have some injuries. That Stephanie is pretty vicious."

"You're pretty tough." He grinned at her. Then his smile faded some. "Tough enough to take some real risks in life."

"Is this another lecture?" She raised an eyebrow.

"No." He paused and met her eyes. "It's just an observation. I just wonder, what other kinds of risks you might be willing to take."

"What do you mean?" She returned his steady gaze.

"Do I really have to spell it out for you, Ally?" He offered her a half-smile. "Just think about it." Ally nodded a little as he stepped out through the door. Charlotte must have noticed her confused expression as she turned back to face her.

"Ally, for such an intelligent woman you really are dumb about some things." Charlotte shook her head.

"Mee-Maw!"

"Okay, you're not dumb, but it's clear that man wants you to take a risk on him."

"Oh!" Ally smacked her own forehead.

"See?"

"Okay, okay." Ally shrugged. "But I don't know if I'm ready, Mee-Maw."

"Only you can decide that, sweetie." She patted her cheek. "But the opportunity may not last forever."

Ally returned to her room after helping her grandmother put the chocolate cake away. She sat down on the edge of her bed. Peaches jumped right up beside her. Ally pet the cat from the top of her head to the tip of her tail.

"What do you think, Peaches? Is it time to take a chance on love?"

Peaches purred and nuzzled Ally's palm.

"Hm. You might be right." Ally bit into her bottom lip and continued to pet the cat. Her grandmother was right, it was a decision only she could make. Her heart had been broken once, and with all that had changed in the past few months she really wasn't sure if she was ready to risk it again.

Chapter Nineteen

The next day when the shop reopened, Ally wasn't expecting much. However, as soon as she slipped the sign to open, Mrs. Cale stepped right in.

"I've been waiting out here for twenty minutes!"

"Oh dear." Charlotte laughed. "Well, I think that earns you some free chocolate." There was a steady stream of customers who happily returned to the shop. Ally was relieved, but she was also proud that their community was ready to rally around them. Maybe it wasn't the city that she was used to, but there was something to be said for the family feeling of a small town. By the end of the day Charlotte and Ally were exhausted, and content.

"See Ally. Nothing to worry about." Charlotte grinned.

"I hear you, I hear you." Ally laughed. "I will

try to have a more positive attitude about things."

"Maybe about your detective as well?"

"He's not my detective, Mee-Maw."

"He could be." Charlotte wiggled her eyebrows.

"Mee-Maw!" Ally laughed.

***

Two days later Charlotte was in her new apartment at Freely Lakes.

Ally set the last box down in the living room and sighed. "Are you sure that you want to stay?"

"Yes Ally, of course I'm sure." Charlotte set a framed picture of Arnold on her mantle right beside a framed picture of Ally and Peaches.

"But you don't even have a room with a view."

"Trust me, I didn't want to get on Ruth's bad side. So, I let her have it. She's been waiting for it longer and wants it more than me anyway. It's not that big of a deal to me, and I'm next on the list when a room becomes available."

"Well, you can always come home. Anytime, Mee-Maw."

"I know that, sweetie." She turned around and opened her arms to Ally. Ally nestled close and wrapped her arms around her grandmother's waist. "You have to stop thinking of this as goodbye, and start thinking of it as hello to a new experience."

"I know, Mee-Maw."

"Maybe you should think about saying hello to another new experience." Charlotte smiled at her. "A romantic one."

"Mee-Maw, it's not like that. Luke just wants to get to know me better."

"Oh honey, I'm not blind and you're not stupid. I'm just asking you to think about it."

"I did romance once, remember?"

Charlotte patted her cheek with the smooth skin of one of her palms. "Don't do that to yourself, sweetheart. Right now you might think you've lived it all, but there's so much more ahead of you, don't hide from it."

"Thank you, Mee-Maw, you know I love you."

"Does that mean you're going to listen to me?"

Ally smiled. "I'll try."

"Good. Now let me get settled into my new place. I'm sure there's inventory and baking that needs to be done at the shop."

"All right, all right." Ally laughed. She hugged her grandmother tight. "I'm just a phone call away. Don't let anyone boss you around. If anyone gives you a hard time..."

"Thanks Mom, I think I can handle it."

Ally shook her head. "I'm sorry, you're right."

"Dinner tonight?"

"Yes!"

"Love you, Ally."

"Love you, too, Mee-Maw."

When Ally walked out of the building she still felt a bit sad that her grandmother had moved out, but she also felt happy for her. When she neared her car she noticed that Luke was leaning against the driver's side door.

"Luke? What are you doing here?"

"I knew today was moving day. I have the day off, so I thought maybe you could use some company."

Ally met his gaze with a light smile. Her heart warmed in reaction to his thoughtful gesture.

"I have some work to do," Ally said.

"I'm happy to help."

"Are you sure?"

"Absolutely." He stood up from the side of the car. "I mean, unless you want to be alone."

"Oh trust me, I'd rather be with you."

"Good." He grinned. "Me too."

As he opened the car door for her Ally couldn't help but wonder if this might just be the beginning of a wonderful new experience.

The End

Decadent Chocolate Cake Recipe

Ingredients:

7 ounces bittersweet chocolate

7 ounces butter

2 teaspoons instant coffee granules

1 cup boiling water

2 1/2 cups all-purpose flour

1 1/2 teaspoons baking soda

3 teaspoons baking powder

1 tablespoon unsweetened cocoa powder

2 cups light brown sugar

3 large eggs

1/2 cup buttermilk

1 teaspoon vanilla extract

For the Chocolate Buttercream Frosting:

7 ounces semisweet chocolate

7 ounces butter

2 cups confectioner's sugar

1 tsp vanilla extract

Preparation:

Preheat oven to 300 degrees Fahrenheit.

Butter and line the base of 2 x 9 inch cake tins.

Slowly melt the chocolate and butter over a low heat.

While the chocolate and butter are melting add instant coffee to one cup of boiling water and set aside.

In a large bowl sift in the flour, baking soda, baking powder and cocoa powder. Stir the ingredients together and then add the sugar and stir again until they are well-combined.

In another bowl beat the eggs. Add the buttermilk and vanilla extract and stir until mixed together.

Gradually add the buttermilk mixture, the slightly cooled coffee mixture and the slightly cooled melted chocolate mixture to the dry ingredients. Stir until well-combined.

Pour the batter evenly between the cake tins. Bake in the preheated oven for 25 to 30 minutes or until a skewer inserted in the middle comes out clean.

Leave the cakes to cool in the tins for about 10 minutes and then remove from the tins and cool on a wire rack. Once cooled remove baking paper from the base of the cakes.

To prepare the Chocolate Buttercream Frosting slowly melt the chocolate in a double boiler.

In a bowl beat the butter until softened.

Gradually beat the sifted confectioner's sugar into the butter. The mixture should be pale and creamy once all of the confectioner's sugar has been added.

Add the vanilla extract and beat.

Gradually and gently stir the melted chocolate mixture into the butter mixture until well-combined.

Spread the frosting over the bottom of one of the completely cooled cakes then place the bottom of the other cake on top to sandwich the bottoms together. Spread the rest of the frosting over the top and sides of the cakes.

Enjoy!

More Cozy Mysteries by Cindy Bell

Chocolate Centered Cozy Mysteries

The Sweet Smell of Murder

Sage Gardens Cozy Mysteries

Birthdays Can Be Deadly

Money Can Be Deadly

Trust Can Be Deadly

Ties Can Be Deadly

Rocks Can Be Deadly

Dune House Cozy Mysteries

Seaside Secrets

Boats and Bad Guys

Treasured History

Hidden Hideaways

Dodgy Dealings

Suspects and Surprises

Wendy the Wedding Planner Cozy Mysteries

Matrimony, Money and Murder

Chefs, Ceremonies and Crimes

Knives and Nuptials

Mice, Marriage and Murder

Heavenly Highland Inn Cozy Mysteries

Murdering the Roses

Dead in the Daisies

Killing the Carnations

Drowning the Daffodils

Suffocating the Sunflowers

Books, Bullets and Blooms

A Deadly serious Gardening Contest

A Bridal Bouquet and a Body

Bekki the Beautician Cozy Mysteries

Hairspray and Homicide

A Dyed Blonde and a Dead Body

Mascara and Murder

Pageant and Poison

Conditioner and a Corpse

Mistletoe, Makeup and Murder

Hairpin, Hair Dryer and Homicide

Blush, a Bride and a Body

Shampoo and a Stiff

Cosmetics, a Cruise and a Killer

Lipstick, a Long Iron and Lifeless

Camping, Concealer and Criminals

Treated and Dyed

Printed in Great Britain
by Amazon